Comhairle Contae
Átha Cliath Theas
South Dublin County Council

LIBRARY SERVICES ONLINE at www.southdublinlibraries.ie

Items should be returned on or before the last date below. Fines, as displayed in the Library, will be charged on overdue items. You may renew your items in person, online at www.southdublinlibraries, or by phone.

South Dublin Libraries
www.southdublinlibraries.ie

D1351732

BLOOD
WILL
HAVE
BLOOD

BLOOD WILL HAVE BLOOD

Catherine Moloney

ROBERT HALE

First published in 2018 by
Robert Hale, an imprint of
The Crowood Press Ltd,
Ramsbury, Marlborough
Wiltshire SN8 2HR

www.crowood.com

© Catherine Moloney 2018

All rights reserved. No part of this publication may
be reproduced or transmitted in any form or by any
means, electronic or mechanical, including photocopy,
recording or any information storage and retrieval
system, without permission in writing from the
publishers.

British Library Cataloguing-in-Publication Data
A catalogue record for this book is available from the
British Library.

ISBN 978 0 7198 2805 8

The right of Catherine Moloney to be identified as
author of this work has been asserted by her in
accordance with the Copyright, Designs and Patents
Act 1988.

Typeset by Chapter One Book Production, Knebworth

Printed and bound in India by Replika Press Pvt Ltd

CONTENTS

To the Three Musketeers,
T, J and P

PROLOGUE

SCHOOLS COULD BE SPOOKY places at the fag end of the day, reflected Jim Snell grumpily as he trundled his caretaker's trolley along the linoleum-covered ground floor corridor of Hope Academy, its squeaking wheels sounding unnaturally loud in the silence.

On the other hand, it was a blessed relief to have the place to himself for a bit after hours of 'yes, sir, no, sir, three bags full, sir.' Those la-di-da teachers with their endless demands simply had no idea, he thought wrathfully. If *they* had to clean up after the little scrotes, it would be a different story, he muttered, skewering a recalcitrant crisp packet with unnecessary venom.

Suddenly he froze mid-lunge, distracted by a hollow clang from somewhere deep within the building.

Though not inclined to flights of imagination, Snell nonetheless experienced a thrill of apprehension.

Seven p.m. on a Friday night. You never saw any of the teaching staff for dust come the start of the weekend, he mused sourly. And all the Facilities Management team should be long gone. The corridor's eau de nil walls, illumined by the security lights outside, had an almost aqueous phosphorescence. Save for the steady thrum of a generator, everywhere was hushed and still.

The caretaker felt an irrational urge to flick the switches and flood all the dark corners with light. Normally he disliked the cacophony of posters which adorned Hope's corridors, clamouring for attention with their headache-inducing primary colours, but in that instant he craved their familiar over-bright assault on his senses.

Could there be a prowler on site, he wondered. Or one of the Year 11 lads messing about for a dare? No, not possible. He would have noticed something amiss on his rounds, but there'd been nothing out of place. Uneasily, he recalled stray gossip about the school 'ghost'. The HR manager had put the mockers on that sharpish, but the memory lingered. Was it possible the place was haunted? Was there some ... *thing* stalking the building?

The moment passed.

Snell told himself to get a grip. This wasn't Friday the thirteenth! Just a leaky, creaky wreck of a sixties building. Likely a mannequin had toppled over in one of the textiles classrooms. Not for the first time neither! Or it could be that wonky grille in the staff elevator – well past its sell-by-date, that was ... Any road, he'd had more than enough for one night. A bottle of whisky awaited him in the caretaker's office, safely hidden away under lock and key in the bottom drawer of his rickety filing cabinet. Time for some well-earned refreshment.

Dry-mouthed with anticipation, Snell cast a desultory eye over the corridor. Nothing stirred. Yawning, he shambled towards the main foyer and his office beyond.

But Jim Snell was not alone. Cat's eyes gleamed in the darkness. A shadowy form glided stealthily from a pool of darkness and moved towards the stairs like a phantom come to take possession of its kingdom. Sighing deeply, as though sucking the essence of the building deep into its lungs, the figure disappeared into the upper regions and was gone.

The nightmare was about to begin.

1

First Impressions

OLIVIA MULLEN SAT DISCONSOLATELY on one of the hideous olive-green 'easy chairs' arranged in rows in Hope Academy's common room on a dreary late October Thursday evening.

Clutching a polystyrene cup of rapidly cooling coffee, Olivia watched her colleagues arrive for yet another interminable staff meeting. As the newest member of the English faculty, she had not yet been whole-heartedly welcomed into any of the departmental cliques which colonized the place on such occasions. The onlooker sees most of the game, she reassured herself, as noise levels rose and a buzz of expectation ran around the room.

Here was dear old Doctor Abernathy, Hope's moth-eaten head of English, bowing gravely to her with old world courtesy. Close on his heels came ginger-haired, cadaverous Mike Synott, the second in department whose whippet-like intensity offered an amusing contrast to his boss's absent-mindedness. Then followed Val Thorpe and Brenda Wray, two sensible middle-aged women, quietly competent with a Mary Poppins air about them. A trio of grungy looking newly qualified teachers, marked by angst and acne, slunk in behind them. Olivia brightened as her old friend Matthew Sullivan, lanky and beanpole-like as ever, sat down beside her wearing his usual expression of ironic detachment.

'What will the dear leader have in store for us tonight, I wonder,' murmured Sullivan mischievously.

'Raising attainment in boys, isn't it?' Harry Mountfield, the rumpled head of religious studies, who had squeezed in next to them, mimed cutting his throat.

'Bit of an oxymoron that,' drawled Sullivan irreverently, eliciting reproachful frowns from Val and Brenda.

Olivia smothered a grin, watching with amusement as Harry proceeded to make himself comfortable. With hayseed hair sticking up in all directions and footballer's thighs akimbo in uninhibited 'manspreader' mode, he was the perfect foil to Sullivan's saturnine elegance. The two men were good friends, generating an air of complicity for which the only word was 'cahoots'. Harry winked at her, and Olivia felt a rush of pleasure at the intimacy, the more so as it elicited a flurry of harrumphing and eyebrow raising from Val and Brenda.

A sudden commotion at the door heralded the arrival of Hope's headmaster, James Palmer – 'call me JP'. Short, balding and perma-tanned, with Eric Morecambe specs, he struck Olivia as curiously charisma-free, an impression reinforced by his squeaky voice and spermatozoon-like physique. 'But don't be fooled,' Sullivan had warned her. 'The man could give Machiavelli a run for his money. He'd stab you in the back as soon as look at you.'

Bobbing obsequiously in JP's wake came the human resources manager and headmaster's PA: Tracey Roach, or 'Cockroach' as she was more commonly known, and Audrey Burke (to rhyme with Berk). Strange, mused Olivia, how a wispy little woman like the Cockroach could wield so much influence. Drearily clad in hues of oatmeal and beige, with an unthreatening grey bob, breathless voice and ingenuous limpid gaze, she was more like a down-at-heel librarian than the power behind JP's throne. Behind the apparently harmless exterior, however, there lurked an arch snoop and world-class sycophant. Certainly, to hear her greasing up to JP was enough to curdle the milk! As for Audrey Burke, her honest, short-sighted eyes shone adoringly at the headmaster from behind bifocals as big as gig-lamps. It was beyond Olivia's comprehension that the woman could not discern what an awful phoney Palmer was. Love was blind *and* deaf in her case!

JP took his place behind a lectern, the Cockroach and Audrey taking their seats in the front row after having conducted a beady-eyed inventory of the room which was now almost full. Any absentees were sure to be slated for a reprimand before the day was very much older.

'Our focus this term is on kinesthetic learning and peer feedback, with a view to helping boys take ownership of their own learning. The Change team will also be developing appropriate intervention strategies for our more vulnerable learners ...'

Same old, same old, Olivia thought glumly, tuning out and contemplating her fellow sufferers. Judging from what sounded like the occasional stifled groan, some of the audience shared her feeling about JP's rhetoric. The poor swots on the front row had it worst of all – recoiling before the heady blast of Paco Rabane, Fisherman's Friend and Capstan Full Strength!

By ironic contrast with the apathy of its captive staff cohort, the common room sported an array of vibrant Day-Glo banners exhorting staff in quasi-religious inspirational terms, *Our Best Always, Everywhere!* being the most egregious example of the prevailing educational esperanto. Survival of the fittest more like!

God, it's an ugly building! Olivia's eyes wandered to the academy's rear courtyard, visible through the floor to ceiling window at the far end of the common room. The modular cinder blocks which enclosed the courtyard on three sides looked even grimmer than usual in the failing light. Matthew and Harry called Hope 'The Bunker', an entirely apt designation for the three-storey cement building situated a little way outside Bromgrove's town centre, next to one of the two municipal cemeteries. *Abandon hope all ye who enter here.*

For the thousandth time, she asked herself what she was doing back teaching English at Hope Academy. Gilbert ('Gil') Markham, her detective inspector boyfriend, had tried to dissuade her from returning to teaching after last year's ordeal at St Mary's Choir School, when she had become involved in a triple murder case. She wasn't sure she fully understood her own motivation. One thing she knew for certain, though. The longer she postponed getting back in the saddle, the harder it would be to rebuild her teaching career. And she still got a buzz from communicating her passion for literature, so it felt too early to pack it all in.

A sharp dig in the ribs from Matthew roused Olivia from her reverie. Uncomfortably, she became aware that Val was fixing her with a hard stare. She did her best to adopt an air of suitably alert interest. Judging from Val's po-faced attitude, her attempt fell woefully short of the mark. It was *so* unfair, she reflected. Only ten minutes or so gone and Harry appeared to be falling into a gentle doze without attracting any similar opprobrium. He'd be snoring his head off in a minute!

At that moment, there was a minor kerfuffle as JP's two deputy heads arrived.

'A thousand apologies, JP. A deputy's work is never done!' brayed Helen 'Killer' Kavanagh (Deputy Head, Curriculum) wearing the expression of abject hero-worship she always adopted on such occasions. Slab-faced and wall-eyed, sporting an unflattering pudding bowl haircut and boxy suit, she resembled nothing so much as a female Khrushchev. The only incongruous touch was her footwear – kittenish ankle-strap stilettos. Of course, it wasn't her taste in shoes which had earned her the nickname 'Killer', though the blood-red stilettos were an apt metaphor for her ruthless ambition.

She wants power so badly you can *smell* it, thought Olivia as she watched Kavanagh plonk herself down on the front row with all the grace of a hippo on safari.

Dave Uttley (Deputy Head, Pastoral), embarrassed to be the focus of so many eyes, sat down next to Kavanagh with a mumbled apology and bashful duck of the head. How on earth had Uttley ever made it onto the Senior Leadership team, Olivia wondered. He might as well have had *Kick Me* tattooed across his forehead. The assertive Vinny Jones 'high 'n' tight' haircut was fatally undermined by a timid goatee and his lips moved continuously, as though he was praying – a not unreasonable assumption given his total eclipse by Kavanagh. And *OMG*, could that possibly be *scrambled egg on his tie*? Emphatically not a look which proclaimed him to be a Master of the Pedagogic Universe!

The common room felt stiflingly hot and stuffy. A wave of exhaustion washed over Olivia. At times like this, she felt that the entire education system, and Hope Academy in particular, was a sodding prophylactic against catching any genuine enthusiasm for literature, culture, or anything else for that matter. The NQTs were yawning and surreptitiously checking the hands of the large wall clock, trying to calculate when their ordeal would end.

'Splendid to hear how colleagues in all faculties are building a climate of mutual respect, trust and co-operation.'

Kavanagh was now on her feet, oozing unctuously. No cliché left unturned. Time to zone out once again.

Olivia let her mind drift. Having only recently returned to the chalk face, it was unlikely that she would be put on the spot ...

Ah, here was another late arrival. But this one sauntered in unapologetically without a care in the world, lounging with languid grace against the wall next to the door.

Ashley 'Dreamboat' Dean. Assistant Head.

The sobriquet was fully justified, Olivia thought as she scrutinized Dean from beneath demurely lowered eyelids. He looked more like David Beckham than ever, bespoke pinstripe suit erotically enhancing rather than concealing a gloriously taut physique – broad shoulders, snake hips, muscular legs.

Taken in conjunction with piercing blue eyes, chiselled cheek-bones, pouty mouth and wavy blond mane (plus tasteful five o'clock shadow), it was little wonder that he had left a trail of broken hearts in his wake.

The staff grapevine buzzed with speculation that Palmer 'had a thing for him'. How else to account for Dean's meteoric rise from groundsman to the dizzy heights of senior leadership? It was unprecedented and had given rise to much muttering in the ranks. Not so much as a GCSE to his name and yet responsible for everything from facilities management to staff appraisal! He *had* to have slept his way to the top!

Little wonder that Jim Snell was glowering sullenly in the corner. Olivia couldn't imagine that *he* had ever lit an erotic fuse. Contemplating the caretaker's wizened figure, she felt as though all the light had been sucked out of him and transferred to his glowing former subordinate. If looks could kill, then she wouldn't give much for the Dreamboat's chances!

Dean invariably appeared oblivious of the Year 10 and 11 Lolitas who lurked in the corridor outside his office in the hope of catching his eye, much to the scowling resentment of their pimply boyfriends. When conversing with the headmaster, he never yielded place to Dave Uttley, despite the weedy deputy head's desperate hemming and hawing as he waited in line. No, Ashley Dean appeared to have eyes only for Palmer, whose physiognomy seemed lit from within, his features irradiated by a glow of pure delight. As though the two of them existed in a magic circle of intimacy from which interlopers were excluded. When Olivia observed them engrossed in their tête-à-tête, the sight made her scalp prickle with an odd sensation of danger. Averting her eyes, she left them to it.

Just when she thought she couldn't keep the rictus smile nailed to her face for a single moment longer, Olivia heard the magic words 'And finally'. Providing some moron didn't ruin things by responding to JP's 'Any questions?' they were home and dry!

For once she was in luck! Even the toadies appeared bludgeoned into silence.

There was a desperate stampede for the door.

'You joining us down the pub, Liv?' This was Harry Mountfield, back in the land of the living and happily anticipating his anesthetic first pint.

'Not tonight, I'm bushed,' she answered truthfully.

As she reached the exit, some impulse made Olivia turn around.

JP and Ashley Dean stood side by side, their heads close together. The look of naked adoration on Palmer's face made her uneasy.

Trouble, she said to herself and slipped away.

2

Olivia

HOME, SIGHED OLIVIA AS she staggered across the threshold of number 56, 'The Sweepstakes', a complex of upmarket apartments at the far end of Bromgrove Park, off Bromgrove Avenue.

Architecturally, the block with its stark cubist lines was something of an anomaly in that part of town, otherwise dominated by down-at-heel Victorian terraces, but Olivia loved the corner flat she shared with Gilbert Markham on the third floor. However toxic her working day, she never failed to be soothed by its tranquil ambience. In an instant, she sloughed off all the small-mindedness, backbiting and petty treacheries of life at Hope Academy. Like a snake shedding its skin, she thought ruefully.

'*In here, Liv!*'

Dumping her bulging briefcase and nimbly side-stepping the islands of books which dotted the carpet and almost every visible surface, Olivia headed for her boyfriend's study.

Markham's sanctum was almost monastic in its lack of clutter. She guessed that the clinical austerity was an antidote to the gruesome effluvia which were his constant companions. No case files, no crime scene photographs were visible, only a police-issue laptop. But Olivia knew that this room, with its view of Bromgrove North Municipal Cemetery, was where her gentle, sensitive lover communed with those whom he had been unable to save, keeping their memory evergreen long after the world had forgotten them and moved on. A striking mixture of hard-bitten worldliness and romantic idealism, it was only with Olivia that Markham ever fully let down his guard.

He turned his white, tired face to her – all its vitality concentrated in quick grey eyes – and pushed the thick, dark hair away from his forehead in a characteristic gesture of impatience.

'Perfect timing, my love. I've had more than enough of crime figures for one day!' He laughed at the expression on Olivia's face. 'Ah, I see it was very bad. Your headmaster not at his Ciceronian best!'

She shuddered theatrically. 'I'd rather have a prefrontal lobotomy than go through that again. It was even worse than usual. We were all sandbagged, but he just chuntered on, spouting the same old mumbo jumbo. Harry Mountfield calls it JP's Esperanto cos it makes bugger all sense to the rest of us.'

Markham's eyes rested lovingly on his girlfriend, the coppery chignon spiralling in wavy tendrils around the flushed face, her slender frame quivering with indignation. She had the uncanny look of another world. *La Belle Dame*

Sans Merci. Yet he knew she possessed a heart as large as that of the Virgin Mary and – for all the philippics against JP and his ilk – an unwavering belief in the essential goodness of humanity.

He always enjoyed her vividly drawn vignettes of Hope's staff and sparkling accounts of the innumerable daily skirmishes with JP and his apparatchiks. But, observing the shadowed eyes and tautly compressed mouth, he felt a sudden sharp pang of concern. Perhaps it had been a mistake for her to return to work so soon, given the trauma of her involvement in the St Mary's murder case. Perhaps he should have tried to dissuade her from returning to Hope Academy where she had previously worked as a supply teacher. Or at least insisted that she go back part-time rather than accepting a full-time permanent position with all its stresses and strains. On the other hand, Olivia was difficult to resist once she had decided upon a course of action. 'I'd only brood and mope if I was at home,' she had told him. 'Work's the best medicine for me.'

Something was bothering her, he shrewdly concluded. Something more than the usual tedious politicking and battles with bureaucracy. Hopefully, she would open up over supper.

Markham's calculation was correct. As they sat over their whisky, having laughingly ranged far and wide over the topics of the day, Olivia returned to the subject of Hope.

'There was a strange vibe in the air tonight,' she said tentatively.

'How so?'

A faint line appeared between Olivia's brows.

'Oh, I couldn't quite put my finger on it, but something felt "off".' She hesitated before adding, 'It's been like that ever since I came back to school. Like when a thunderstorm's brewing and the air's so muggy that you get a headache ...'

'So, you think some sort of scandal might be about to break?' enquired Markham with a chuckle. 'How delectably improper!'

Olivia grimaced. 'Well as to that, I don't know... At first I thought people might be wary of me because of ... everything that happened last year, but then I realized it wasn't that.'

Markham waited expectantly.

'D'you remember my telling you about the new assistant head?'

'The one you call the Dreamboat? Meteoric rise from pool attendant or some such...?'

'Groundsman,' Olivia amended with a smile. 'Yes, that's the one.'

'What about him?' Markham was gratifyingly curious.

'His name's Ashley Dean. Word has it he leapfrogged his way to the top of the promotion ladder all because JP has a pash.'

Markham was thoughtful. 'Isn't the head married? A family man?'

'*Was.* He and Cheryl separated last year.'

'Because of this infatuation?'

'It's beginning to look like it ...' Olivia groped for words. 'Oh, I feel prurient saying this ... but there's definitely something weird going on. You should have seen the way JP was looking at him. Totally smitten.'

'Hmmm. And does young Mr Dean return his affection?'

asked Markham with mock-primness.

Olivia pulled a face. 'He's what you'd call an operator. Cut quite a swathe through the staff – male and female – leaving emotional havoc in his wake.' Seeing that Markham was watching her closely, she added softly, 'Not *me*, Gil. I saw through him from the start. There's something *vulpine* about him,' she shuddered, 'a sort of animal instinct for scenting vulnerability. He was downright cruel to Audrey Burke. I told you about her, didn't I? She's the head's PA and number one fan. Well, Ashley christened her 'the galloping gormless' and mimicked her all the time.'

'Didn't you tell me he'd had a tough childhood? Something about a violent father?' The assistant head's biography had resonated with Markham, scarred as he was by unspeakable experiences at the hands of an abusive stepfather.

'That's right. He's not had it easy.' Olivia was, typically, anxious to be fair.

'For all the gaps in his formal education, he's got real street smarts and ambition … It's just …' She twirled a strand of auburn hair around her fingers in a distracted manner. 'He's dead behind the eyes, you know. Like Archie Rice. Dead behind the eyes.'

'How does he treat the students?'

'I wouldn't be surprised if he hadn't played his little mind games with one or two of them.' Olivia's voice took on a distinct edge. 'I remember an incident when I was doing supply. I saw a Year 10 boy come blundering out of Ashley's office – he was facilities manager then. The lad was all red-faced and awkward, but what I remember most is the sound of mocking laughter floating out into the corridor. I just *knew* Ashley had wound that boy up somehow. Adolescent insecurities would make pupils fair game in his book. And he was clever enough to know which ones would be too embarrassed to say anything.'

Markham's face revealed that his detective's antennae were twitching.

'Oh no, dearest,' his girlfriend was swift to reassure him, seeing that his thoughts had travelled to the young victims in the St Mary's murder case. 'Nothing like St Mary's. The child protection honchos will never get him for anything. He's far too smart for that.'

'So, he's likely just using JP to get ahead, then? Unless it's a case of blinding physical attraction... But I thought you said JP was first cousin to Quasimodo and all that.'

'I don't think I went quite that far!' Olivia spluttered.

'No, *now* I remember. You said he could star in a remake of *The Mummy* without any need for cosmetics.' Markham's tone was teasing.

'*That was Harry, not me!*' Olivia looked somewhat shame-faced. Then she rallied. 'Well, there's no denying that JP's punching above his weight. Ashley's drop dead gorgeous. On past form, I'd say he's stringing JP along for venal reasons.'

'Hope's version of the casting couch, then,' said Markham. The keen grey eyes scanned Olivia. 'So, that's what's creating all the undercurrents, is it? This romantic imbroglio between the head and assistant head?'

'I honestly don't know, Gil.' Again, that faint line between the brows. 'It's as if Ashley's a vortex for all sorts of negative feelings swirling around. But there's something else too.' She sipped her drink before continuing. 'At the meeting tonight,

I felt real *hate* in the common room ... *By the pricking of my thumbs, something wicked this way comes.*' She laughed shakily. 'Don't worry, dearest, it's just my PTSD kicking in. C'mon, I'll do the washing up followed by a spot of cathartic marking. It's 9TB tonight. TB standing for *Thick as Bisto!*'

Markham tactfully refrained from further questioning, but inwardly he resolved to keep a closer eye on Olivia. At least Matthew Sullivan and Harry Mountfield were watching her back. He felt sure his girlfriend's self-appointed praetorian guard would alert him if anything untoward threatened.

Later that night, while waiting for Markham to come to bed, Olivia switched on her laptop to wade through the day's emails.

Scrolling through the endless messages, she noted uneasily that many of the emails emanated from Ashley Dean. What in God's name was JP playing at? It was one thing for the headmaster to give his arm candy the 'decorative' role for which he was so pre-eminently suited, but quite another to cede him this kind of executive power.

Hearing Markham's study door close, she shoved the computer to one side.

Tomorrow is another day!

Bromgrove Police Station was a building of surpassing drabness, reflected Markham on Friday morning at 6 a.m. as he contemplated the beige lego-brick complex. Same school of architecture as that bunker where Olivia worked.

He lingered, savouring the cold, still air, postponing his encounter with the fug of CID, looking across from the station to the soot-streaked Victorian gothic edifice of Bromgrove

Town Hall. The terraced cemetery of St Chad's Parish Church rose behind the Town Hall on one side, with Hollingrove Park gently undulating into the distance on the other. It was a pleasing outlook on a late autumn morning. For a moment, he wished passionately that he could betake himself to one of the park benches and enjoy an interval of solitude and utter repose.

The moment passed. Squaring his shoulders, he passed through the revolving doors into the station foyer, briskly acknowledging the greeting of the desk sergeant before heading for the lift which would take him to CID.

The open-plan space was quiet, only the strip lighting and dodgy water cooler humming quietly in the background. Some tired Swiss cheese plants were dotted around at strategic intervals in a desperate attempt to ameliorate the prevailing sterility, but somehow this poignant attempt at indoor landscaping merely accentuated the room's claustrophobic stuffiness. Markham had a glassed-in corner office with narrow louvred windows offering unparalleled views of the station car park. Deftly, he flicked open the blinds which screened the glass partition walls.

Open for business!

Right on cue, DS George Noakes ambled through the door, bearing what Markham assumed was some death-by-cholesterol offering from the canteen. As usual, he looked as though his clothes had been pitchforked on with absolutely no attention paid to overall effect. Today's combination was particularly bilious, comprising a mustard tweed jacket teamed with a less than pristine blue shirt, maroon regimental tie and baggy off-white trousers. Olivia had been delighted by what she termed Noakes's 'psychedelic' dress sense, but Markham's superiors remained distinctly unimpressed.

'For God's sake, Markham,' DCI Sidney had hissed after a recent briefing, 'do something about your DS. He's an absolute disgrace. Sets an appalling example to junior officers.'

And yet, for all the professional opprobrium that the obdurately un-PC grizzled veteran invariably attracted, Markham stubbornly resisted any attempt to banish George Noakes to Siberia. Only he knew how much he owed to Noakes's unflashy dependability, compassion and common sense. Only he knew how well each acted as the other's counterpoise. Eventually, DCI Sidney (or 'Slimy Sid' as he was popularly known) and Superintendent Collier had given up trying to detach Noakes, though not without dire prognostications on the potential damage to Markham's chances of further promotion.

He was willing to take the risk.

'Morning, Guv,' Noakes grunted, plonking himself down on one of two sagging armchairs in front of Markham's desk. Without further ado, he proceeded to unwrap his polystyrene cargo, revealing a lurid burger and hash browns liberally spattered with ketchup.

Markham sighed, wrinkling his nose fastidiously and doing his best to suppress a wave of nausea at the overpowering smell of grease.

Such was their morning ritual. Set in stone as far as Noakes was concerned.

Noakes stole a furtive glance at the discreet framed picture of Olivia on Markham's desk – the only personal touch in the office save for a few nineteenth century classics on the bookshelf. His attitude to Olivia was a mixture of awe and apprehension. Privately, he thought she was like one of those sorceresses from his daughter Natalie's childhood picture books sprung to life. Fascinating, mysterious, other-worldly – so no wonder the DI was struck all of a heap by this red-headed will o' the wisp. They were well-suited, to his mind, despite her being five years older. Noakes didn't understand half of what she said, but he liked listening to the sweet, musical contralto and watching the green eyes glow with enthusiasm. And she was good for the boss – had softened some of his edges and banished the haunted look from his eyes. Noakes rarely shared personal confidences with the notoriously reserved Markham, whose austere demeanour repelled any attempt at over-familiarity. But by some alchemy of their curious sub-oral communication, he knew instinctively that Olivia was the DI's soulmate and that without her he would take to bleeding inwardly.

'What can you tell me about Hope Academy, Noakes?'

Noakes prided himself that he was rarely taken by surprise, but the startled expression on his battered features showed that the question came out of left field.

'Well, Guv, I know your ... Olivia ... well, I know she teaches there, an' I don't want to speak out of turn ...'

'That generally doesn't bother you, Noakes,' came the dry response, 'so no need to spare my delicate sensibilities.'

'Well, it's got a bit of a reputation, Guv. Kids out of control, if you know what I mean. Some real tearaways. I'm just glad our Natalie went to Bromgrove Secondary. They've got their priorities right there.'

Having spied Noakes's daughter out and about in Bromgrove's less salubrious nightspots, Markham privately reckoned that Natalie was making up for lost time, however, he kept his counsel and made vague noises of agreement.

Mollified, the DS said, 'Not that I'm saying the teachers at Hope are all useless, mind.' *Perish the thought.* 'That Harry Mountfield's sound. Plays five-a-side with some of the lads from uniform.'

'Yes, he's one of the good guys according to Olivia.'

Emboldened, Noakes expanded further. 'I've been up there from time to time with PC Doyle from the Community team. Didn't much care for all the higher-ups, to be honest.'

Markham repressed a smile. 'I believe they're called the Senior Leadership team these days,' he said in mild reproof.

The DS snorted contemptuously. 'Bloody ridiculous. In my day, there was the head an' deputy head an' folks knew what was what. Now they've all got these fancy titles and are too grand to spend any time in the classroom. My Muriel says—'

Markham hastily cut him off at the pass, being only too well acquainted with the worthy Mrs Noakes's views on the iniquitousness of public institutions from the government down.

'No scandal or anything like that then, Noakes?'

'Nothing to speak of, except for a young maths teacher who left in a bit of a hurry.' The DS added lugubriously, 'Usual sort of thing, boss. Some girl had a crush on him then started shouting the odds. She broke down and admitted it was all moonshine, but he scarpered anyway.' He scratched his head thoughtfully, 'The head was a real slime ball, dead insincere.'

Markham subsided into a brown study broken by Noakes enquiring, 'Why d'you want to know about Hope, Guv? Summat wrong there?

'Oh, just something that came up in conversation with the Police Commissioner,' the DI replied vaguely.

Noakes understood that whatever was troubling the boss, he would learn nothing more for the present. Markham would revert to the subject when he was ready.

At that moment, there was a tap on the door.

'DC Kate Burton reporting for duty, sir!' said a cheerful treble.

As Markham and Noakes stared blankly at her, the bright smile wavered.

'On secondment from Family Liaison, sir. DCI Sidney said you were expecting me.'

'*Of course!*' Markham's voice sounded unnaturally hearty to his own ears, but he was anxious to make the eager new arrival welcome, especially given Noakes's marked lack of enthusiasm.

DC Burton wore a sharply pressed, gender-neutral taupe trouser suit and crisp white shirt with Nehru collar which made her look like an upscale communist. Her neat conker-brown bob framed a broad, button-nosed face only redeemed from absolute plainness by its air of alert intelligence.

Markham waved the newcomer to the vacant armchair next to Noakes's, observing with amusement the way she carefully dusted it down before perching gingerly on the edge as though fearful of catching something. Much to Noakes's evident stupefaction, she then whipped out a notebook and pen, looking at the DI with a rapt attention that bordered on reverence. From the bulldog-chewing-a-wasp expression on his DS's face, Markham knew that he was busily inventorying Burton's indictable offences. *University graduate. Leftie. Tree-hugger.*

Keen as mustard. Brown noser. Plain bloody annoying.

The DI suppressed the urge to groan. Whoever had assigned Burton to his team had a warped sense of humour. The chances of the DS reining in his inner neanderthal were vanishingly small. The best he could hope for was that the new DC's visible determination to make a good impression was proof against anything Noakes could throw at her.

'Right,' he said, inwardly wincing at his own avuncularity and ignoring Noakes's smirk, 'let's get on with it. There was that GBH on the Hoxton yesterday. Take PCs Doyle and Davies with you and report back to me soonest.'

Noakes's mouth turned down at the corners, but Markham ignored his evident displeasure and added meaningfully, 'You can show DC Burton the ropes, Sergeant. By way of, er, induction.'

Burton visibly perked up at the mention of induction, though Markham had only used the word because the new recruit looked like the kind of officer whose preferred bedtime reading was *Blackstone's Police Manual*. Noakes's snort was eloquent in its repudiation of such niceties.

After they had left, Markham found himself unable to settle. Restlessly pacing his office like a condemned man facing the drop, the DI's thoughts kept coming back to Hope Academy and Olivia's misgivings.

History couldn't repeat itself, could it? She had been through so much last year, with those horrible murders at St Mary's. The scar tissue had only just formed over those old wounds, leaving her raw underneath. When she screamed in the night, he knew which ghosts stalked her because they pursued him too.

He'd get the Community team to do a discreet recce. Hadn't Noakes mentioned that Hope was on PC Doyle's beat? Yes, Doyle and Burton could pay a visit tomorrow – do a talk on drugs or some such as cover for sniffing around and getting the lie of the land.

The decision made, Markham reluctantly turned his attention to the day ahead. Miss Purcell, his punctiliously correct PA, was no doubt hovering in the vicinity.

Hope Academy would keep.

3

A Discovery

FIVE P.M. ON FRIDAY afternoon.

After a day of frenzied mayhem, Olivia was trying to keep a low profile.

Located at the far end of the English wing, her classroom E1 was on the third floor of the 'bunker', with a bird's eye view of the Children's Memorial Garden in Bromgrove South Municipal Cemetery. She never failed to be touched by the array of brightly coloured balloons and inflatable toys bobbing above the marker stones in a gallant display of pride and commemoration. On her very worst days, when past horrors threatened to overwhelm her, these poignant offerings reminded her of the indomitability of the human spirit.

What will survive of us is love.

Standing by the window, she was smiling at two new *Noddy* and *Brambly Hedge* tributes and congratulating herself on having dropped off the senior leadership team's radar when there was a gentle tap at the door. Suppressing a sigh, Olivia called, 'Come!'

Her head of department Doctor Abernathy stood irresolutely in the doorway, subfusc looking even more shop-soiled than usual, spectacles sliding down his nose and the shock of white hair standing on end as though he had spent the last hour running his hands through it in an ecstasy of abandonment. Anyone else would have barged in, Olivia thought, but not the doc. The man belonged to a different era. She noticed he was emitting those beaver-like noises he tended to make when he had something difficult to say.

'Miss Mullen,' he began softly before grinding to a halt.

Olivia beamed encouragingly at him. He was *such* a dear man, totally unsuspicious that Hope's senior leaders looked askance at his old-fashioned ways and were busily measuring him for his professional shroud.

'Miss Mullen,' he said pathetically, waving a crumpled sheaf of paper with a distracted air. 'I fear I am behindhand with various administrative tasks including some data entry for Year 11.'

Olivia could well imagine it, since he notoriously found digital media as impenetrable as Hindustani.

'I allowed myself to become distracted by Doctor Donne,' was the shamefaced excuse. 'Time ran away from me ...' He trailed away into a series of inarticulate sounds

Typical Abernathy. From anyone else in the department, it would have sounded deeply suspect, but not from him.

'No problem at all, Doctor Abernathy,' she reassured the old man whose lack of guile and prurient curiosity had been pure balm amidst the twittering and impertinent nosiness which had accompanied her return to Hope. 'Leave it with me. I can easily put it on the system.'

'That is most kind of you, Miss Mullen!'

Abernathy looked as though the weight of the world had been lifted from his shoulders. Ramming his spectacles back to the top of his nose, he darted forward and thrust the wad of paper into Olivia's outstretched hands before pirouetting on the balls of his feet and trotting away to his office at the opposite end of the landing. No doubt he would soon be blissfully re-immersed in *The Complete Works of John Donne*. Good luck to him, she thought, contemplating his retreating figure with affection. It would be terrible if JP, 'Killer' Kavanagh and co succeeded in replacing him with some whippersnapper who could talk fluent baloney with the rest of them!

The thought of Hope's senior management team had a galvanizing effect on Olivia. It was getting late and darkness was stealing over the memorial garden.

Time to make a move.

She hadn't been quick enough!

At that moment, Helen 'Killer' Kavanagh bustled in through the door that Abernathy had left open and, without waiting for an invitation, plonked her ample form down on a desk at the front. Olivia marvelled that it didn't disintegrate beneath her.

'Olivia, I'm always *so* impressed by your professionalism. No shooting off on the dot for *you*! *Unlike some of your colleagues.*'

There was a pregnant pause. Clearly this was an invitation to bitch. But Olivia wasn't biting.

'Well, actually, I was just about to call it a day myself,

Helen. All work and no play, you know ...'

The other bulldozed on regardless. God, thought Olivia, she was like some awful juggernaut. Programmed to bore the pants off anyone unfortunate enough to cross her path.

'... omissions in the English faculty's behaviour sweep.' The woman finally paused for breath.

Wondering irritably why the hell Killer always said *faculty* rather than *department*, Olivia's gaze fell on the large stash of buff folders and computer printouts the deputy head was clutching to her capacious bosom.

Rewinding the monologue to which she had been listening with only half an ear, she realized belatedly that she was being dumped on from a great height.

Certain colleagues, it now transpired, had buggered off without completing some bureaucratic BS that was apparently urgently required.

'But I *knew* you could be counted on to help plug the gaps.'

Skewered by Kavanagh's gaze, Olivia desperately tried to think of a pressing commitment elsewhere. And failed.

'Splendid!' the deputy head boomed, spraying her with copious amounts of spit. 'It should only take a couple of hours.' (*Hours!*) 'And of course, it's a feather in your cap. A real plus in terms of making up some of the ground you lost during your ...' She paused with ostentatious delicacy. 'Sabbatical.'

In the circumstances, Olivia felt she could dispense with that particular honour. Trust Kavanagh to identify the weak point in her professional armour. As usual, however, she was helpless in the face of the other's remorseless momentum. Ignoring Olivia's piteous look of mute appeal, the deputy head manoeuvred her bulk off the desk with surprising agility (now that it was mission accomplished, thought Olivia savagely) and sailed towards the door.

'I'd have stepped in myself but for the Governors' Meeting tonight. You know how it is!'

Oh yes, I blankety-blank well know how it is, screamed Olivia inwardly, finding some relief in assorted profanities as she raged against the unfairness of it all. Trust bloody Kavanagh. Skipping off on Smarm Patrol (the leopard-print stilettos always came out on such occasions) while leaving her to sort out yet another departmental cock-up. At least the deputy head hadn't managed to catch poor Doctor Abernathy red-handed in the act of abdicating his administrative responsibilities. Then it really would have been a case of blood on the carpet. Nature red in tooth and claw!

Glumly, she gazed out at the gathering dusk.

There goes my precious Friday evening down the swanny!

Eventually Olivia calmed down sufficiently to recall that it would be hours yet before she saw Markham. Wearily, she plugged in her ancient kettle and made some black coffee in the only one of her mugs that didn't resemble a still life with fungi. Times like this really called for a minibar, but caffeine (and lots of it) would have to do. Muttering wrathfully to herself, she set her shoulder to the wheel. Kavanagh owed her for this big time and, for once, she was going to make sure she called in the debt.

Some considerable time later, Olivia sat back and massaged her aching shoulders. Her head throbbed and her eyes were gritty with weariness. She glanced at her watch.

Nine p.m.! OMG!

She checked again to make sure. But there was no mistake.

Those 'omissions' Kavanagh had airily mentioned turned out to be more like great gaping chasms.

A little chill ran down her back.

Nine p.m. meant that the Facilities Management team would have closed up for the night. Which meant that she was locked in! For some reason, no-one had checked her end of the wing as per the Facility Management team's usual procedures.

Olivia opened her door and peered out. All was still and silent. Without students and staff, the building resembled a submarine, fathoms removed from the upper world. The distant hum of traffic from beyond the cemetery sounded like the distant swell of ocean breakers, a sinister lullaby putting the school to sleep.

What was that? Blinking myopically, jolted out of her trance, Olivia was sure she had seen a shadow detach itself from the wall and whisk around the corner, moving sinuously in the direction of the stairs at the far end of the corridor.

'Hello. Is anyone there?'

She felt decidedly foolish croaking from the door of E1. But something – she couldn't say what – had caused the hairs on the back of her neck to stand on end. She just had a gut feeling. Something was terribly wrong.

Perhaps Doctor Abernathy was still in his office communing with John Donne. It wouldn't be the first time that the delightfully impractical head of English had been locked in. Gliding down the corridor like a ghost, she paused outside his office.

It was a forlorn hope. The good doctor was gone for the night.

Her head whipped round. *Shit*! Wasn't that the lift?

Yes, she could hear its creepy automated voice and the soft whoosh of closing doors. Someone else was definitely in the building with her. Someone who didn't want to be seen.

Enough, she told herself firmly before walking cautiously down the stairs.

She checked the second floor landing and corridor, then the first.

Finally, she reached the ground floor. The lift appeared undisturbed, the cage in its usual position, no lights flashing or anything else amiss. And yet, she was sure she had heard it travelling between floors.

All clear.

But Olivia still had a sixth sense that something was off-centre. She was so used to the *feel* of the school – like a shabby overcoat which moulded itself to her body – that she instinctively sensed something in the atmosphere had shifted. It was as if some noxious substance, as deadly as any stored in the science department's fume cupboards, had escaped and was on the loose.

She shuddered. This was getting ridiculous, she admonished herself. Less *Stephen King* and more *Home and Garden* for her in future! Taking a deep breath, she asked herself what Markham would do.

Right, she would go back up to her classroom and call that miserable git Jim Snell on her mobile. He would come over all 'belligerent of Bromgrove' on her, but it couldn't be helped. Any port in a storm.

Leadenly, her ears pinned back for signs of anything unusual, Olivia trudged back up the stairs to the third floor.

And came up short.

She felt her chest tighten, her breath catch.

About halfway along the corridor was a dark bundle as though someone had curled up on the floor and was sleeping.

Shrinking against the wall, feeling her way along with her fingers, she inched closer.

A mannequin. With some sort of purplish mask over the face.

What, she wondered in bemusement, was one of the props from drama doing up here on the third floor?

Oh dear God in heaven. The metallic smell of blood should have alerted her. This was no prop.

A body. And somebody had smashed the face to a pulp.

Olivia reeled backwards in horror. *Don't you dare faint*, she muttered, wrapping her arms round her shaking body, her nails digging into the skin hard enough to draw blood.

Breathing in shallow gasps through her mouth, she crouched down beside the body.

It was the signet ring on his pinkie, not the gleaming blond hair nor the made-to-measure suit, which told her who it was.

The Dreamboat. Ashley Dean. The man she had seen only that afternoon laughing his handsome head off with JP as they stood together, thick as thieves, in conclave at the door of the headmaster's office. And now her premonition had come to pass. Somebody had silenced the arrogant laughter for good.

The face was unrecognizable. Olivia could feel the hatred behind the obliteration of Dean's features.

Forcing herself to look further down, she saw with horror that the crotch too was a sea of blood. Mutilation. *Oh dear God in heaven.*

Olivia began to feel as though she was floating above her own body and observing the grotesque scene from above. *Shock, I'm in shock.*

For all she could tell, the murderer might still be in the building. *My phone, I've got to get my mobile and call the police*, hammered the insistent refrain in her head. But still she crouched there transfixed. A sound that she did not recognize as her own voice seemed to reach her from somewhere a long way away, sobbing and moaning, as if in the grip of a bad dream.

Eventually, shaking all over, Olivia found herself back in E1. Afterwards, she had no recollection of making the journey from the third floor abattoir to her classroom, nor of calling 999 and Markham. The rest of the evening passed in a blur of blue lights, screaming sirens and practised hands lifting her gently into an ambulance.

'Please, not with his body!' she begged, and they seemed to understand.

The last thing she remembered before the prick of a doctor's needle was Markham's powerful tender hand taking her cold fingers in his and the well-beloved voice soothing her with calm authority.

'We'll take it from here, darling Liv. We'll take it from here.'

Bathed in its sullen after hours nimbus of pallid neon, Bromgrove Police Station looked deceptively quiet from the outside. CID, by contrast, was a hive of activity, with officers scurrying about creating an ad hoc Incident Room. The dejected-looking Swiss cheese plants received short shrift.

'Get those bloody creepers out of here!' yelled Noakes, sprawled across his workstation and dunking a Krispy Kreme doughnut into a mug of creosote-strength coffee. 'You can dump 'em on "Titchmarsh" Taylor in Vice!'

Finally, an array of whiteboards, consoles, maps and telephones had been scrambled to his satisfaction.

'Cheers, lads,' he declared, 'you've done a great job. We'll sort the office manager an' indexers tomorrow morning with the guv.'

As the office emptied, DC Burton came panting into the room, closely followed by PC Doyle, both wide-eyed with excitement at the prospect of a real-life murder investigation. Burton's eyes were the size of enormous brown lollipops, while Doyle's open carroty face was even more flushed than usual.

Kate Burton was breathless with enthusiasm. 'Is it true there's been a homicide at Hope Academy, Sarge?'

'That's about the size of it,' replied Noakes, very much the inscrutable old-timer whom nothing could discompose.

'Is it true that DI Markham's girlfriend found the body?' blurted Doyle. 'What's she like? Is she a stunner like the fellows in Traffic say? Wasn't she involved in the St Mary's murders last year?'

Observing the air of quiet desolation which stole across Burton's face at these questions, Noakes smiled to himself. *So, that's the way the land lies.*

In a manner suggestive of the ancient family retainer guarding his master's secrets, Noakes loftily kept his counsel. 'Not my place to say. The boss'll tell you what you need to know.'

In truth, the DS felt oddly protective of Markham and

Olivia. He well knew the DI's loathing of 'canteen culture' and vividly recalled the way Markham had shrunk from exposure of his fledgling relationship. Despite himself, he had been stirred by Olivia's grace and tender solicitude for her policeman lover. Something about the way she looked at Markham brought a lump to Noakes's throat. It had been a long time since anyone had looked at *him* like that.

The swing doors to CID whooshed open, and suddenly Markham was striding towards his office, crooking a finger for the team to follow.

With a heavy sigh, he flung himself into the chair behind his desk, causing its springs to squeal in protest.

'How's she ... er, the witness ... er, the lady who found the body ... doing?' Noakes felt it incumbent on him to speak first.

The DS's ponderous attempts at discretion were wasted.

'No need to beat about the bush, Noakes.' Markham shot him a wry smile. 'Olivia's fine, thank God, just badly shocked.' His hands gripped the arms of the chair so that the knuckles stood out white. 'Having found the body, she's potentially at risk, though. The message needs to go out loud and clear that she didn't see or hear anything.'

'Roger that, Guv.' Noakes was stolidly reassuring. He glared at the two younger officers, as though they might have been tempted to disagree and cleared his throat. 'Have we got ID on the victim, Guv?'

'The assistant head, one Ashley Dean.' Markham's features contracted at the memory of that butchered corpse. 'It was a bloodbath,' he added sombrely before shaking himself. 'Look, you should get off home. I'm just going to write an initial briefing note for DCI Sidney. Yes,' in answer to

Noakes's interrogative look, 'they're letting me take charge of this one though the DCI's technically SIO. It could be a can of worms if the gentlemen of the press get a whiff of Olivia's involvement. So, for God's sake, *no leaks!*' Markham's tone was fierce. Burton and Doyle nodded mutely before heading for the door as one.

Noakes lingered. 'Will you be all right, Guv?'

Markham made a shooing gesture. 'Get some shut-eye, Noakesy, I'll see you bright and early. There's something really nasty about this one, so we need to hit the ground running.'

After the DS had left, Markham switched off the light in his office and sat brooding in the darkness.

Olivia had been right. There was something foul and mis-shapen concealed at Hope Academy. Pray God he could bring every secret into the light and, above all, keep Olivia safe.

4

Aftermath

MID-MORNING ON SATURDAY, MARKHAM and Noakes sat in the DI's office reviewing developments. Noakes was aware that the DI had already visited the hospital to check on Olivia, but refrained from raising the question of her return to Hope. For all his lack of refinement, the DS was capable of surprising sensitivity where Markham was concerned. The boss would get around to the subject of his girlfriend when he was good and ready.

The DI ran his eye down the assignments sheet. 'So, you've left Burton and Doyle down at Hope with the Forensics teams.'

'Yeah, they're down there getting the feel of the place an' rustling up an office for us, Guv,' Noakes grunted in between slurps of coffee that had the consistency of sludge.

As the DS savoured his caffeine hit, Markham mentally reviewed what he knew about Kate Burton. Having read DCI Russell's reference, he had followed up with a telephone call on the basis that there was nothing like the personal touch.

'She'll go far, Markham,' boomed the genial head of Family Liaison. 'Good academics. 2.1 from Reading in psychology, which should prove useful. Ultra-conscientious and does her paperwork. Had a fight to get here.'

This sounded intriguing.

'How so?'

'Burton's an only daughter. Parents had her late in life, so very overprotective. She won her mum round to the idea – took her along to one of the community open days, which scuttled a few myths – but her dad wouldn't budge, at least not for a long time. I gather he's still not happy – wants her in a nine to five job or safely married off.'

'God, that's antediluvian, sir.'

'Well, I've got some sympathy with the man. He's ex-military, saw active service abroad and was treated for combat stress.'

'Ah, I see. Doesn't want her in the front line.'

'Something like that. Though, from what I hear, you fast track youngsters end up desk-bound most of the time.'

'Ain't that the truth, sir,' Markham said with a wry smile.

'I think she'll prove an asset, Markham.' The DCI was brisk now. 'Just so long as that sergeant of yours doesn't send her screaming for the hills, eh.'

'Noakes is my secret weapon, sir.'

'Well, no other department's clamouring for him.' Russell's voice was dry. 'And if Sidney gets his way, he'll be put out to grass before long.'

Over my dead body.

'Anyway, let's look on the bright side, shall we? If Burton

can deal with Noakes, she can deal with anything.'

It sounded like a challenge ...

Back to the present.

'Burton seems to have her wits about her,' Markham said mischievously. 'The report from DCI Russell describes her as highly efficient with the makings of a first-class officer.'

'Oh aye.' Noakes was clearly underwhelmed. 'That one's so sharp she'll cut herself one day,' he commented laconically. The corners of his mouth turned upwards in a sly smile. 'Seems a bit star-struck an' all, what with working under you.'

'Hmmm.' Markham was never comfortable with references to his celebrity status and swiftly reverted to the matter at hand. 'So, there were quite a few staff around despite it being the weekend?'

'A fair crowd. With Dean being a local lad, news got around fast.'

'What did you make of Hope's senior leadership team?'

The DS rolled his eyes expressively.

'There was this godawful woman. Helen Kavanagh. Built like a brick shithouse with voice to match. Kept banging on and on about mental illness an' security in schools. Obviously hoping to pin this on a local loony.'

Markham grimaced. 'I don't buy it. The murder was planned. *Personal.*'

'Yeah, well.' Noakes scowled at the grubby stub of paper covered in his great looping scrawl. 'After I'd gone ten rounds with Godzilla, I had a quick word with the other deputy head. Weedy little bloke, name of Uttley. Looked too scared to say boo to a goose. Bet he has a hell of a time with Kavanagh. All the time I was talking to him, she was giving us the evil eye. He didn't look like a murderer to me, but then you can never tell with the runty ones ... just look at Crippen—'

'Did you get any sense of how they got on with Dean?' Markham cut in impatiently.

Noakes was derisive. 'Nah. It was all that "He-Didn't-Have-An-Enemy-In-The-World" bollocks. Pass the sick bag.'

'What about the head, James Palmer?'

'Now that *was* interesting.' Noakes's head came up like a hound scenting its quarry. 'Last year, when we were checking out Hope after the scandal with that young maths teacher, I thought Palmer was dead phoney. I mean, all that "call me JP" stuff for starters.'

Intriguing, thought Markham, the way Noakes echoed Olivia's verdict on Palmer.

'He behaved like we were in some sort of TV cop show,' Noakes continued, warming to his theme. 'Kept using cheesy phrases like *mano a mano*. God, it was awful. Carried on like we were a team. Hope's answer to NYPD Blue!'

'And today?' Markham prompted.

'He was a wreck. Absolutely in bits. Couldn't have been more upset if it was his nearest and dearest. Had tears running down his face when he was talking to me. Godzilla was glowering, but he didn't seem to notice. Kept saying "Why Ashley?" and "It doesn't make any sense." To be honest, I thought he was going to keel over.' The DS gave a sudden grin. 'Then there was this dotty old chap wandering around. Only one of 'em wearing a batman gown like teachers used to wear back in the day. Doctor Aber ... something or other.' Noakes consulted his bit of paper. 'Oh yes, that was it. Doctor

Abernathy.' He chuckled. 'The old fella kept offering everyone cups of tea. Or something stronger "for medicinal purposes". It was priceless. I thought Godzilla was going to nut him!'

Markham's careworn expression momentarily vanished. 'Sounds like we can rule out Doctor Abernathy.' He laughed.

'Not necessarily,' Noakes said ruminatively. 'From what I heard, the knives were out for him. Management trying to show he was past his sell by date an' putting him down the whole time. Must've been humiliating. Ashley did most of the bullying from the sound of it. So, you see, Guv, mebbe the worm turned and Abernathy finally snapped. You never know with those quiet types ... may look as if a puff of wind would blow him over, but ...'

'True. Appearances can be deceptive.'

It occurred to Markham that disaffected former teachers might also have a motive for murder if they had been culled because of Ashley Dean's machinations. Something for Burton to get her teeth into.

Noakes looked cagey. Clearly there was something else.

'Come on, spit it out.'

'Palmer's reaction was a bit OTT, guv. Abernathy looked dead shifty when I commented on it ... Could he and Dean ... well, you know ... could they have been, like, *at it?*' The DS blurted out the enquiry with his trademark lack of finesse.

'I had the impression from what Olivia said that JP and Dean may have been,' Markham chose his words carefully, 'particularly close.'

'Like I said, *at it!*' Noakes was hugely delighted with his own perspicacity.

'We don't know anything for sure, Noakes.' Markham's

tone was stern. 'So, for God's sake don't charge in there shouting the odds.'

''Course not, boss,' came the obedient reply. 'But,' Markham steeled himself for something outrageous only to be confounded by the reasonable enquiry, 'if they *were* in a ... *relationship* an' it went wrong ... couldn't that give us motive?'

'Yes, it could,' the DI replied bluntly. 'But it's early days.' He exhaled slowly. 'What about other staff? Did you get a chance to speak to any of them?'

'Difficult with Kavanagh watching them like a warder. The HR manager ...' Noakes looked at his notes. 'Tracey Roach started blubbing, but it didn't look like the real thing from where I was standing. Audrey Burke – she's the head's PA – was rabbiting on about Palmer needing a doctor. I had the feeling,' Noakes observed shrewdly, 'she was worried about him shooting his mouth off to us.'

'Hmmm.' Markham steepled his fingers and contemplated the DS thoughtfully. 'I think we'll get you to interview those two, Noakes.'

The other nodded sagaciously. 'They're sure to know where the bodies are buried.'

Markham winced, but Noakes was cheerfully oblivious.

'Who'll you take, Guv?'

'Kate and I will do the teachers.'

'Figures,' Noakes said glumly. 'What with her having a university *ed-u-ca-tion.*'

Only Noakes, thought his boss, could make the DC's graduate pedigree sound like a disadvantage!

'Oh an' there was a caretaker hanging around as well. Jim Snell.' Noakes screwed up his nose in distaste. 'He looked like all his Christmases had come at once. Must have *hated* Dean, who was something special in the looks department apparently.' Noakes continued his tale with dramatic relish. 'It was all a bit weird, Guv. Dean started out at Hope as a groundsman, under the caretaker. Basically, Snell's skivvy. Next thing, he was assistant head bossing all the support staff about. Ended up as Palmer's right-hand man, busy poking his nose into everything.'

That tallied with Olivia's account, thought Markham.

'Bit of a step up, wasn't it, Guv?' Noakes was like a dog with a bone. 'Bog cleaner to big cheese. Him and Palmer *must've* had something going.'

Markham frowned. 'For God's sake, don't let anyone hear you talking like that. We don't want the rubber-soled lot on top of us.'

'Mum's the word, Guv. Right, I'll get back down there.' The DS assumed an expression of Confucian inscrutability comically at odds with the enormous postprandial belch with which he signed off their conversation. Markham watched ruefully as his subordinate headed for his afternoon's tasks by way of the station canteen. No doubt he would raise hackles left, right and centre before the day was done. But that was what the case *needed*: someone to go in, mix it up and hopefully catch Ashley Dean's colleagues on the raw.

There had been something viscerally intense about this murder, reflected Markham uneasily, rifling through the scene of crime photographs: the victim's face pounded to the consistency of chopped liver ... the ghastly mutilation. As though the killer had been in the grip of some terrible blood lust which nothing could satiate.

Suddenly the office felt unbearably hot. He strode across to the window and wrenched it open, welcoming the cold breeze gusting in from outside.

After a few minutes, he returned to his desk, his thoughts turning to Olivia. The blood rushed to his face as he recalled DCI's Sidney's conversation the previous night.

'Of course, *technically* your girlfriend is a suspect, Markham.' Only Sidney could lace the word 'girlfriend' with such salacious innuendo, the DI thought savagely, his hands balling into fists. What followed was even worse. 'Misfortune seems to, well...' falsely bonhomous laugh, '*follow* her. Almost as though she's *jinxed*, poor soul. I mean, after that ... ahem ... *awful* affair at St Mary's, it's such an *appalling* stroke of *bad luck* that *she* should be the one to find the body.' Markham felt as though poisoned weapons were being hurled at him. *Saint Sebastian shot with arrows.* He absorbed Slimy Sid's vindictiveness in mute rage, trusting that the DCI would eventually tire of his little game. And so it proved, Sidney exclaiming peevishly, 'You can investigate this one, Markham. But as my second in command. Is that clearly understood?'

The DI had not trusted himself to speak but Sidney barely noticed, satisfied that he had put the rising star of Bromgrove CID firmly in his place.

As for Olivia, at the hospital that morning, she had mourned Ashley Dean with heartfelt and transparently genuine sadness.

'I didn't really like him, Gil, but nothing could ever justify *that*.' She shivered like a whippet then whispered, 'He was so very beautiful, with a kind of aura about him ... as though he was untouchable, invincible ... *Golden lads and girls all must,*

As chimney sweepers come to dust.' The nurse had regarded her patient warily before agreeing that Olivia could be discharged that afternoon once the duty registrar had given the all-clear.

Markham glanced at his watch. Time to get going. He would collect Olivia, see her comfortably settled at The Sweepstakes and then check in with the team at Hope.

He wondered if the murderer was there too, watching the police at work. Watching and waiting.

'Bloody hell, sir, I bet Clintons are quids in today!'

Markham and a police constable stood and stared at the carpet of cards, balloons, soft toys and flowers which blanketed Hope Academy's front courtyard in an eerie facsimile of Bromgrove South Municipal Cemetery on the other side of the school drive.

'Just like when Princess Di snuffed it,' breathed the young officer reverentially.

Markham was emphatically not a fan of emotional incontinence. Yet there was something poignant about the display. All the messages, with their ribbons, butterflies, cuddly animals and other embellishments, showed that many grieved sincerely for Ashley Dean.

Watched respectfully by his youthful subordinate, the DI bent down and picked up a particularly lurid condolence card, which bizarrely featured Winnie the Pooh, Piglet and Eyore as chief mourners. *We miss you, sir, but will remember you forever.* Hardly deathless prose but, despite himself, Markham was moved. Whatever the man's flaws, he had touched some young lives for the better.

Although Hope was closed to students for the day, Markham spotted a gaggle of older girls clustered around a sapling in one of the flowerbeds which bordered the courtyard. On closer inspection, they appeared to have constructed some sort of impromptu shrine to the assistant head whose megawatt smile and sultry smoulder, captured in a large photograph pinned to the tree, offered eloquent testimony to his sobriquet of 'Dreamboat'.

There was something comically awkward about the big-haired bejeaned teenagers posing for selfies next to the 'memorial', tears streaking their Polyfilla-thick make up and oompa loompa fake tans. Spotting Markham and his sidekick, the sobbing coven retreated towards the car park at the end of the drive.

'Keep tabs on them, will you, Constable,' Markham instructed, 'and if any press turn up, just refer them to the press office. Thank God it's the weekend, so at least security won't be too much an issue for now.'

As his colleague headed towards the car park, Markham remained where he was, contemplating the school's ugly frontage.

Not enough light, he thought, looking at the rows of meanly proportioned windows in Hope's soulless sixties prefab. He wasn't all that keen on the current craze for clinical modular design and glass atriums – too antiseptic by half – but at least the newer schools didn't resemble battery farms.

He was so wrapped up in his own thoughts, that it was some minutes before he noticed that he had company.

Recognizing Harry Mountfield, Olivia's friend and head of religious studies, Markham shook hands cordially. The big untidy man, with his prop forward's build, always struck him as bursting with vitality.

'Horrible, isn't it?' He laughed, jerking a thumb at the building. 'Like a cross between a women's prison and a branch of B&Q.'

'Pretty grim,' Markham concurred. 'I can see why you might get cabin fever working in a place like this. Maybe you'll strike lucky in the next round of government spending and get something dazzlingly futuristic.'

Mountfield pulled a face. 'Like a spaceship, you mean. Beam me up, Scotty!'

Markham smiled. He could see why Olivia relaxed around her colleague. There was something endearingly subversive about him.

They fell silent.

'How's Liv?' asked Mountfield simply.

'Badly shaken up, as you can imagine.' Markham's tone was sombre. 'She won't be in school for a few days.'

'I should hope not ... Did she ... *see* anything?' Mountfield caught himself up short. 'Sorry, you're probably not allowed to say.'

'No, that's OK, Harry. She doesn't remember a thing that happened before she woke up in hospital. Must have been so traumatic, that she blanked it all out.'

'Probably for the best. Poor Liv,' the other murmured, gnawing his lower lip.

There was another, longer silence. Following the direction of Mountfield's gaze, Markham noticed he was staring at the schoolgirls' shrine to Ashley Dean, the murdered man's charisma overwhelming even in death.

At that moment, a small knot of people emerged from the front foyer. One man detached himself from the rest, descended the steps and walked over to the improvised tribute. Head bowed, he stood motionless, apparently lost in contemplation.

Mountfield made a disgusted noise in his throat, quickly repressed.

Markham looked at him interrogatively.

'That's James Palmer, the headmaster. Marvellous thespian instincts.' The tone was bitter.

'You don't like him,' Markham observed bluntly.

'Oh, don't mind me. I'm a dinosaur, Inspector. JP's one of the new breed of "executive heads".' Mountfield's air quotes hung in the air like a challenge.

'What's one of them, then?' the DI enquired mildly.

'More interested in budgets and spreadsheets than anything else. Able to spout politically correct bullshit by the bucketful and great at buttering up local authority VIPs, but no clue how to relate to the kids. Twat of the first order.'

Markham whistled. 'That's quite a rap sheet! Any redeeming qualities?'

'Not so's you'd notice.' He gestured towards the group watching Palmer from the top of the steps. 'He's made some bloody awful appointments too. Well, you'll meet Cruella de Vil in a minute.' Markham noticed a beefy female with a corrugated blonde haircut eyeing them suspiciously. 'Yep,' sighed Mountfield resignedly, 'here she comes.'

This must be the deputy head Helen Kavanagh, Markham thought as the woman clip-clopped towards him on spindly maroon suede stilettos. The one Olivia called 'Killer' Kavanagh. Her high colour clashed unbecomingly with a violent fuchsia suit, while the fixity of her stare made the DI feel as though he was about to be swallowed whole.

Mountfield melted away, moving remarkably swiftly for such a big man. Clearly, he had no wish for a heart-to-heart. Kavanagh's eyes narrowed as she followed his retreating figure, leaving Markham in no doubt that the antipathy was mutual.

Gravely, Markham held out his identification for the deputy head's perusal.

'*Of course, Inspector!*' she trilled in an affected falsetto. '*I know you by reputation, though I don't believe we have ever met.*'

I'd have remembered *you*, he thought dourly.

Sensing that she was about to launch into a pre-prepared speech, Markham forestalled her.

'I don't want to intrude on your grief today, Ms Kavanagh.' Killer immediately assumed an appropriately doleful expression. 'But I'd like to get all the staff into school for tomorrow if possible. I realize that's a tall order with it being Sunday, but it means we can do interviews with minimal disruption to the running of the school. Obviously, we'll need an office from Monday ...'

The deputy head waved a regal hand. 'Your people are already installed.' Markham mentally apologized to whichever hapless member of staff had been turfed out to accommodate them. 'As for calls to the workforce, I'll put that in hand immediately.'

The DI decided some shameless flattery was called for.

'I knew I could count on your efficiency, Ms Kavanagh.'

The doughy features creased in a smile of gratification.

'Happy to be of service, Inspector. Whatever it takes to ensure this ... this *maniac* is taken off the streets.'

It was nicely judged. Kavanagh was obviously determined to steer them away from Hope Academy – preferably in the direction of the Newman, the local high-security facility situated behind Bromgrove General Hospital.

'Oh, I don't think we want to jump to any conclusions, Ms Kavanagh,' he said firmly. 'Important to keep an open mind at this stage.'

To the DI's immense relief, a figure appeared at Kavanagh's elbow.

'*JP!*'

Markham regarded the head with interest. The man appeared ill, his eyes bloodshot behind the heavy black-rimmed spectacles.

'Good afternoon, sir,' he said gently. 'I'm very sorry to be here on such business.'

Palmer looked as though he was seeing Markham from a long way off, his eyes unfocused.

'I can't feel Ashley anymore,' he whispered tremulously. 'He's gone. *Gone!*'

With a combination of shoulder and arm, Helen Kavanagh moved and manipulated her distraught colleague away from the DI towards the steps which led to the foyer. 'I think we need to get you home, JP.' To Markham she mouthed the word *Doctor!*

Markham let them go and once again looked thoughtfully up at Hope's façade.

A *façade* is what it is, he decided. Like a stage-set.

Time to bring the actors down towards the footlights.

5

Mourning Rites

THE REMAINDER OF SATURDAY passed uneventfully, Markham leaving Noakes and Burton, along with PC Doyle, to secure the school and ensure their temporary office had everything needed.

Back at The Sweepstakes, he told Olivia, 'I'm pulling up the drawbridge, dearest. DCI Sidney and the rest can go whistle. *You're* my priority tonight.'

Over a roast chicken supper, he regaled her with a mock-humorous description of the students' mourning rites, and was pleased to see a flare of amusement in the tired eyes. Her features tightened, however, when he described the encounter with Helen Kavanagh.

'Killer didn't care for Ashley one bit,' she told Markham. 'Thought he was a jumped up little oik with ideas above his station.'

'You make Hope sound like Downton Abbey,' Markham commented dryly, bringing a smile like pale wintry sunshine to the careworn face.

'Well, it's true schools *are* very hot on hierarchy. It's all about the pecking order and sucking up.'

'Not a million miles from CID,' he murmured. So far, his plan to distract Olivia from her sad thoughts was proving effective.

'Dean seems to have been spectacularly good at sucking up,' he continued. 'From what staff told Noakes and Burton, he played Palmer like a fiddle.' Observing the fleeting look of revulsion on her face, he said, 'Don't speak ill of the dead. I know. But Ashley Dean aroused strong passions, dearest. Clearly some people *detested* him.'

'There was a lot of jealousy because he came from nowhere.'

Markham looked at her expectantly.

'And he did a lot of the head's dirty work. JP's obsessed with paring budgets to the bone – mad keen to cull anyone past their sell-by date.'

'Like Doctor Abernathy.' Markham smiled, recalling Noakes's description of Abernathy's eccentric behaviour.

'Exactly. Even though he's the salt of the earth and been there for years. I mean, Gil,' said Olivia with increasing passion, 'how could *anyone* have it in for the doc? All right, he lives in his own little world, but he's a gentleman – never says a bad word against anyone. Even when JP and Ashley kept dropping in to "observe" him, scribbling away on clipboards and poncing about in their smart suits like Hope's creepy answer to the Blues Brothers, he never took umbrage. Always scrupulously polite even when Ashley sneered to his face. There was just one time when I saw the doc's hands trembling. And then, I tell you, I wanted to *kill* Ashley!'

Markham sent up a prayer of gratitude that no-one else was present to witness Olivia's vehemence.

Suddenly realizing what she had said, Olivia flushed and fell silent. Observing her downcast expression, Markham prompted, 'Do you think resentment at Ashley's meddling could have spiralled into something more deadly?'

'Not with Doctor Abernathy, no.' She looked thoughtful. 'But Ashley certainly had plenty of enemies. It was that cruel streak of his, you see.'

'He and Helen Kavanagh were two of a kind, then?' The deputy head had struck Markham as ruthless.

'Oh God.' Olivia sounded disgusted. 'That android! Charges around trying to brainwash people with PC gibberish like something out of *The Manchurian Candidate*.'

Markham burst out laughing.

'I'm not sure the lady and I exactly hit it off.'

'You and the rest of the western hemisphere! I don't know how Dave Uttley stands it. Poor sod gets a hand bagging every day—'

'More like a stiletto in the heart,' Markham interjected as he thought of Kavanagh's footwear.

Olivia's eyes crinkled with delight. 'Yeah, you figure she'd be into Hillary Clinton pantsuits but it's kitten heels or bust! Freud would have a field day!' Her face suddenly clouded over. 'Somehow I've survived, Gil, but it's no thanks to Goneril. She's always sniping about my "dramatic escapades" ... makes me sound like some kind of nut case!'

Markham forbore to mention that DCI Sidney engaged in very similar rhetoric.

'You don't see Kavanagh as a murderer, then?' he enquired

with airy casualness.

Slowly, Olivia shook her head. 'She's poisonous all right. But despite her nickname, I can't imagine her losing control like that. Her weapons are character assassination and innuendo.' She added with a shudder, 'There was something so *passionate* about the way Ashley was killed. As though someone wanted to obliterate him from the face of the earth.'

Markham sensed her mind was travelling down dark by-ways.

'Just one more question, Liv, and then we can batten down the hatches and have a box-set binge.'

'Ask away.'

'Is there anyone on the staff you think might be capable of violence like that – if pushed too far, say?'

Olivia looked down at her plate with its half-eaten supper, seemingly lost in thought. Then she looked across the table with childlike earnestness.

'I honestly can't think of anyone, Gil, though there was lots of muttering in corners. Matt called Ashley a twat once. And Harry told him to stick his clipboard ...'

Markham grinned. Matthew Sullivan's waspish sense of humour had enlivened many an evening at The Sweepstakes, and Harry Mountfield was clearly cut from the same cloth.

'I get the gist,' he drawled. 'Hope's senior leaders are used to subservience, aren't they? *When I say jump, you ask how high.* But there's no bowing and scraping from those two!'

A light broke through the gloom of Olivia's face. 'That's why they're my best friends,' she said simply.

'*Right!*' Markham got up from the small oval table where they had dined, gesturing her across to one of two tartan high-backed armchairs waiting invitingly on the other side of the room. 'Doctor Markham prescribes mindless entertainment, my love,' he said with gentle warmth, 'so dig out a DVD while I make coffee.'

'Anything I like?' she asked happily, rising too.

'Hmm, within reason. Let's rule out Scandi noir and anything with subtitles,' Markham replied, enfolding her in his arms and kissing the top of her head. 'How about *Downton?* Let's disappear behind the green baize door for the evening.'

The following morning saw Markham slipping out of The Sweepstakes bright and early.

Wreathes of mist were slowly breaking up, allowing cold clear sunshine through. Listening to Sunday bells chiming across Bromgrove, Markham was filled with nostalgia for the time when he was a regular churchgoer. A lapsed Catholic, it was as if the corrosive loss of innocence had somehow outlawed him from his faith.

Long-forgotten lines of poetry rose unbidden to his mind and, for a moment, he was back in the lower sixth form, listening to one of his Jesuit instructors in full spate.

"I fled Him, down the nights and down the days; I fled Him down the arches of the years; I fled Him, down the labyrinthine ways Of my own mind."

Sometimes he accompanied Olivia, a practising Anglican, to St Chad's. But whenever he tried to raise his thoughts to Heaven, he felt the gates were firmly closed and bolted against him. As though he was too tainted by sordid experience to receive spiritual consolation. As though the ghosts of numberless dead clung to him and would not let him move out of his cold, dark tunnel into the light.

'Don't worry,' Olivia told him with touching certainty. 'One day the fog will lift.' Maybe, he told himself, her arrival in his life heralded the advent of hope and a time when those tightly barred gates would swing open. In the meantime, while all the familiar landmarks might have disappeared, he could at least continue to fight for those whose wrongs cried out for justice.

Once he arrived at Hope, Markham sank low in his car seat and watched as the staff arrived in gaggles of twos and threes. All appeared subdued and self-conscious, looking apprehensively over their shoulders as if they suspected the car park of being bugged.

Burton drew up in her Mini Metro, followed by Noakes and Doyle together.

'I wonder how Ms Mullen's doing,' Doyle said as the DS carefully locked the Ford Mondeo, his pride and joy, keeping a wary eye out for any teenage tearaways who might be lurking.

'Wouldn't ask the guv, if I were you, lad,' grunted Noakes. 'He's very buttoned-up about his private life. No Entry signs all over the shop.'

However, Noakes's thoughts were also running on Olivia. She doesn't look a teacher, more like a hippie or a witch, was his first thought when Markham introduced them. Wonder if she dyes her hair that colour, was his second. My Muriel'd say she isn't the full shilling, he ruminated. Can see why a bloke would get ideas, though – you could drown in those big eyes.

But for all the DS's bewildered susceptibility to Olivia's rare brand of enchantment, he was doggedly loyal to the guv'nor and bristled when anyone – including DCI Sidney

– made snide remarks, reacting as though such insults were reptiles to be throttled and flung off. All that mattered was she was good for the guv'nor. The rest of the world could mind its own business.

Turning his thoughts back to the present, the DS noticed that Doyle looked distinctly down in the dumps.

'What's up?' he prompted. 'You've got a face like a wet weekend.'

'It's Sally,' came the glum response.

'Given you the heave-ho again, has she?'

'Summat like that.'

Noakes drew himself up with something of a Churchillian air.

'Now come on, lad, you can't bring your love life to work.' He lowered his voice conspiratorially, gesturing meaningfully at Kate Burton. 'Leastways not when Miss Goody Two Shoes is sniffing about for all the best jobs.'

The DS had a genuine affection for the young PC, despite his gormlessness.

'You're a local boy, an' we don't want outsiders having it all their own way. So, look lively and show the DI that you're as good as any university hot shot.'

Doyle started to look more cheerful.

'D'you really think there's a chance of me moving to CID, Sarge?'

''Course I do.' Noakes slapped him on the shoulder. 'But not if you're drivelling over that bossy little besom instead of keeping your mind on the job.' He leered affably and gave the younger man a portentous wink. 'Save it for the pub. I'll give you some tips on your love life then.'

'There's the DI.' Doyle sounded livelier now.

Together the two men headed over to where the tall dark figure was standing, DC Burton in close attendance.

Markham was clearly impatient to get on with the day's work.

'Right,' he said, 'First stop the LRC, whatever that is—'

'The Learning Resource Centre, sir,' chipped in Burton.

'Good. We're meeting all the staff there for a briefing. Then we'll get started on interviews.'

He led the way towards the foyer, where the tinted plate glass obscured what lay beyond.

As the electronic doors of the main atrium swooshed shut behind them, they were assailed by a breathy whisper.

'Can I help you, officers?'

The speaker was a drab little woman who seemed to have materialized out of nowhere. A lanyard proclaimed her to be the HR manager, Tracey Roach (aka 'Cockroach', recalled Markham, casting his mind back to Olivia's account). Dressed in some sort of dreary beige caftan-cum-twinset, she stood with arms outstretched so that, for one appalling moment, Markham feared they were being invited to participate in a group hug. The moment passed, however, and she ushered them towards the Learning Resource Centre (why on earth can't they just call it the library, wondered Markham irritably) wittering away about the 'devastating loss to our family'. He felt a pang of compunction at his uncharitable reaction, reminding himself that grief manifested itself in widely different ways: it did not necessarily follow from Tracey Roach's gush of words that she was insincere.

Waiting at the door of the LRC was the head's PA Audrey

Burke ('The Berk'). Looking at the red-rimmed eyes which peered myopically up at him through hideously ugly bottle glasses, Markham felt instinctively that he was in the presence of genuine distress. Fear too. Nervous fingers pleated her cheap skirt into tight folds and she kept glancing over her shoulder, looking furtively through the glass panel of the LRC door as though to check the whereabouts of something or someone. The Cockroach briskly manoeuvred the policemen past her fluttering colleague and into the LRC.

Too much time in this place and I'd have a thumping migraine, thought Markham, as he absorbed the colour-coded posters which adorned every spare inch of wall space. Exhausting, not restful, he concluded.

Helen Kavanagh bore down on them. Out of the corner of his eye he observed PC Doyle clocking the kinky footwear with fascinated interest – Jimmy Choos, from the look of it, totally inappropriate for her scrum-half's build.

While Killer droned on, Markham scanned the staff whose haggard faces seemed leached of colour by the glaring hues of the LRC's decor. Thanks to Olivia's entertaining, and unprintable, descriptions of Hope's *dramatis personae*, Markham was able to place many of them.

The teaching staff appeared to be seated by department. Markham easily recognized Doctor Abernathy, a Gandalf clone whose decrepitude made Noakes look positively dapper by comparison. Next to him sat a ginger-haired, cadaverous young man who looked like a cross between DH Lawrence and a heroin addict. That had to be the second in department, Mike Synott. A couple of sturdy women were eying up the hapless Synott as though they fancied him for lunch.

Furthest away from Abernathy and co sat the minor satellites – presumably newly qualified teachers or juniors. Matthew Sullivan, lounging against a bookcase behind the group, met Markham's eyes with a look of weary complicity. This is going to be a production and a half, his expression seemed to promise.

There was no sign of James Palmer.

God, when was Kavanagh going to come up for air? The unpalatable truth was that Ashley Dean had most probably been murdered by someone from the school, quite likely one of those sitting quietly at that moment in the LRC.

Gathering from Kavanagh's pious platitudes about the 'sad increase in random violence,' she was still hoping to steer the police firmly in the direction of local mental patients.

Kavanagh was on a hiding to nothing, decided Markham. With his extrasensory awareness of danger, he knew he felt evil right there in the kiddie-friendly setting of the LRC.

From what Olivia had told him, this murder was the work of someone who knew the school and the victim – someone who had stalked his or her prey, staked out the killing zone and staged the gruesome tableau into which Olivia had stumbled. He would have to ensure the school jungle drums broadcast the fact that she remembered nothing of that night and was too traumatized for any attempt at regression therapy. Otherwise she could be in danger. Spotting the stocky, rumpled figure of Harry Mountfield at the table just next to the English team, Markham thought he could count on Olivia's friend to help with that. He noted with amusement that Mountfield's face wore an expression of startled incredulity which deepened as Kavanagh really hit her stride and began denouncing 'The Selfish Society' for its lack of compassion towards 'those on the margins'.

Markham decided that he'd heard enough. Any more of this twaddle and Kavanagh would be suggesting he cut out the middleman and head straight to the Newman to conduct interviews there. Case closed!

He cleared his throat, halting Kavanagh in her tracks.

'We're keeping an open mind at this stage, Ms Kavanagh. All lines of inquiry will be vigorously pursued.'

The deputy head appeared to be getting her second wind, so he continued hastily, 'What I want to do today is conduct preliminary interviews with all teaching staff along with DC Burton whom I believe some of you have already met. My colleague DS Noakes will be speaking to support and administrative staff.' My God, he thought, was that hard-faced harpy at the front with the fearsome nail extensions actually getting out a *compact* to check her make-up? Wait till she clapped eyes on Noakes!

The other deputy head, the wimpy one, Dave Uttley, was mumbling about having a room ready for them. The man looked terrible, bad eczema giving him the look of a Pointillist portrait gone awry. There were great dark bags under his eyes which bore a haunted expression. Of course, that could be accounted for by present company. Godzilla had to be the coadjutor from hell!

Now Uttley was introducing the caretaker Jim Snell. Markham caught a sour whiff of whisky and sweat and decided that he didn't much care for the man; a shifty, weaselly little customer and no mistake. What was it Olivia had called him? Belligerent of Bromgrove? Well, the fellow certainly had a surly puss on him – he must have *hated* Ashley Dean leaving him in the dust as he whizzed up the promotion ladder!

Markham made a mental note to do some digging into Snell's antecedents, then followed Kavanagh, Uttley and the caretaker along a claustrophobic warren of corridors to a small office. Giving it a quick once-over, he decided it had all the essentials (most important – certainly as far as Noakes was concerned – being a kettle and fridge). Kavanagh seemed inclined to linger, but PC Doyle, catching Markham's eye, scotched the deputy head's plan for a cosy *tête à tête* with the Senior Investigating Officer, politely ushering her out into the corridor. Trailed by her hapless lieutenant and Snell, she left them to it.

'It's a bit dark and poky, sir.' DC Burton gestured apologetically around the cramped space whose three desks – two crammed up side by side against one wall with a third jutting out awkwardly from the other wall into the middle of the room – showed signs of having been hastily vacated, piles of manila files and paperwork pushed aside and the odd grungy mug left behind. The one meanly proportioned window looked onto a strip of gravel which bordered some straggling bushes and sparsely planted flowerbeds, their etiolated shrubs contributing to the melancholy aspect. Beyond the flower beds was a stretch of scrubby grass ending in a block of four netball courts. Even these looked tired and unloved, with their faded grid lines and potholed surfaces, festooned with crisp packets and burger wrappers. As Markham watched, Jim Snell appeared, his mouth set in a grim line, heading for the courts with his litter picker.

All in all, not the most prepossessing billet. Even on the

brightest day, the sun's rays would never cheer it. At that moment, a breeze whipped up outside, sending the thin leaves into a kind of frenzy before suddenly subsiding when it hit the building. As though something about the school struck a chill even into Nature, the DI thought uneasily.

'At least that HR woman knows how to look after visitors. We've got tea, coffee, milk an' chocolate digestives, Guv.' Noakes, as ever, was focused on the claims of the inner man, plonking his booty down on a tiny, verdigris-encrusted sink at the back of the office to the left of the window. Ignoring Burton's disapproving gaze, he set about brewing up while PC Doyle disinterred some mugs from a dusty cupboard next to the sink.

Markham was just resigning himself to the pit stop when there was a timid knock. Dave Uttley's head appeared around the corner of the door.

'Would this be a convenient time, Officers?'

Markham nailed an encouraging smile to his face. 'Of course, Mr Uttley.'

'Dave, please.' Uttley advanced into the room as though about to face the firing squad.

Markham noted the sheen of perspiration on the deputy head's upper lip and his nervous hand-wringing. Once again, he was struck by how ill the man looked. *Need to go gently with this one*, the DI told himself.

'Let's have a cuppa before we get started,' he announced reassuringly. 'DS Noakes can do the honours.'

As a manoeuvre to help Uttley relax, the tea-making was useful. The man was so wet you could wring him out, but Markham felt a twinge of sympathy. Working in harness with a ball-breaker like Kavanagh was guaranteed to drain the life out of anyone.

After some anodyne chit-chat about the ever-changing educational landscape, Markham moved up a gear.

'Would it be fair to say that Ashley Dean isn't going to be universally missed?'

A flush worked its way up Uttley's neck.

'There *were* some concerns that he wasn't qualified for the position of Assistant Head, Inspector, because he hadn't come through the ranks in the usual way.'

'Did *you* like him?' asked Noakes bluntly.

The flush became painful, but Uttley's gaze was steady and his response candid.

'No, I didn't, Sergeant. I think he carried baggage from the past which made him treat people quite ruthlessly. He was what you might call a schemer.' The deputy head paused for a moment and then added bitterly, 'I was certainly taken in by him at first. He was so charming to my face, that it took me a while to realize he was undermining me behind my back.' He shrugged. 'All part of his empire-building, I guess. The head was very taken with him.'

Markham decided not to beat about the bush. 'Word on the grapevine is that there was something going on between James Palmer and Ashley, which is why he shimmied up the career ladder in double quick time.'

Uttley had clearly been expecting this. 'I'd heard the rumours, Inspector, but there's no hard evidence for anything like that. Schools are always gossip-mills and it could just have been jealousy. Or maybe the teachers and TAs (teaching assistants, he translated for Markham's benefit) didn't like him lording it over them.'

'What with them being *professionally qualified*, you mean?' Noakes's tone made his opinion of academia abundantly clear.

'Something like that,' was Uttley's mild response. He ran a finger inside his shirt collar as though it suddenly felt too tight. 'Look, I don't pretend to understand the dynamics, Inspector, but speaking personally, I never witnessed any impropriety between Ashley and JP.'

After they had taken details of Uttley's whereabouts on the night of the murder – at home, comatose in front of the box with no 'significant other' able to vouch for his movements – Markham sent him on his way. As the door closed behind the deputy head, the DI reflected that Uttley's comments about Dean's manipulativeness tallied with something he remembered Olivia saying. 'Ashley had Dave Uttley and Audrey Burke eating out of his hand, imagining they were his new BFs.'

'BFs?' Markham struggled to follow her shorthand.

'Best Friends. He used and abused them. Took what they had to give and then dropped them. Used private stuff they'd told him as his party piece for staff bashes.'

The question was whether the dead man had wound Dave Uttley up to the point of no return.

No, decided Markham, they couldn't rule out Uttley. Physically unprepossessing he might be, but it did not preclude his being a murderer.

Hell hath no fury like a deputy head systematically belittled.

An assertive rat-tat-tat on the door heralded the arrival of the other deputy head. Helen Kavanagh sailed in without waiting to be invited and plopped down into the chair vacated by Uttley.

'I'm sure Mr Uttley will have told you that the next assistant head will have some pretty big shoes to fill, Inspector.'

Markham blinked. God, that was quick! Back there in the LRC, Kavanagh couldn't shut up about Ashley Dean being irreplaceable. Now she'd segued smoothly to the topic of his replacement! No-one is indispensable, he thought. Particularly not at Hope Academy. The gleam in the deputy head's eyes belied her earlier rhetoric about irreparable loss.

Markham realized that Kavanagh was quite capable of hijacking the interview. Time to lay on the flattery with a trowel while heading her off at the pass.

'I believe you have a BSc in psychology, Ms Kavanagh. Taken with your considerable professional experience, I'm sure you can offer the police some valuable insights. You'll appreciate that we have to consider the school environment as well as the wider community, so it would be useful to have your personal impressions of Ashley Dean.' From the way the deputy head preened, Markham knew that this appeal to her vanity had been successful.

'Ashley was commendably ambitious and proactive. If I had one *teensy* criticism, it would be that he overextended himself. Facilities management was his area of responsibility, but he was keen to get involved right across the board – behaviour, teaching, PR, staff training, everything really.' Her expression hardened. 'Obviously, with his primary remit being *maintenance*, it was difficult to keep all the balls in the air at once.'

Markham allowed himself a swift exchange of glances

with Noakes. He could read the DS's mind. Translated from SLT-speak, this meant that Kavanagh thought Ashley Dean was a presumptuous upstart and she *hated* the way he tried to muscle in on her brief. As far as she was concerned, he was Mr Ronseal and had no business strutting around in pinstripes as if he owned the place.

Markham decided to stir things up. 'The head must have seen leadership potential in Ashley.'

Something like real hatred flashed across Kavanagh's face, quickly veiled. Dropping her voice by a couple of octaves in the manner of a seasoned tragedy queen, she murmured huskily, 'Poor JP! Under *such* pressure, private life a bit of a shambles, and, between you and me, struggling to cope. Perfectly understandable that he became over-dependent on Ashley.'

Oh, she was quite an operator, thought Markham with reluctant admiration. No vulgarly explicit reference to sexual shenanigans between Palmer and Dean, just the unmissable suggestion that Palmer was having an identity crisis with all that this implied. Try as he might, he couldn't get anything more out of her. Technically she appeared alibied for the night in question, having been at a meeting until 8 p.m. and then out to supper with two of the governors (sucking up, presumably). Still, he had the very distinct feeling as the interview progressed that Kavanagh wanted to steer them away from Hope. Why?

'What the hell was going on with the head and Dean?' Markham burst out in frustration after Kavanagh had departed with the smug air of one who had put the police in their place. 'Was it some dark secret from their past which bound them together? Was Dean playing mind games with the head? Or blackmailing him?'

'Could well've been, Guv,' the DS replied phlegmatically. 'He was good at holding things over people apparently. Clearly Kavanagh thought he was a poisonous little Johnny come lately.'

'Jim Snell would agree with her there.'

'I've checked Snell's background, sir,' said Burton eagerly. 'Two previous for assault, but they were domestics and he didn't do time.'

'That fits,' was the DI's response. 'Snell looks like a woman-beater rather than the kind of man who'd square up to another bloke.'

'What if he flipped?' pressed Burton, blushing at her own temerity. 'Must have hurt losing out to someone like Ashley with movie-star looks and patter to match.'

Humph, thought Noakes, noting the way Burton drank in Markham with her eyes, her colour rapidly coming and going. *She's got it bad.*

'I just don't see Snell for this, Kate.' Markham's brow corrugated as he thought back to the murder scene. 'Whoever did it was clever enough to have blindsided Ashley Dean and slipped away like a thief in the night. He – or she – is out there now mimicking grief and manipulating the whole situation. Snell doesn't have that kind of subtlety.'

'Ashley was into power tailoring all right.' Doyle sounded wistful. 'His wardrobe's like something out of *GQ*. Talk about dressed to kill.' He gave an embarrassed laugh. 'Sorry, unfortunate turn of phrase, sir. But seriously, he must have been high maintenance. His flat's like Bling Central.'

'Hmm, I wonder,' Markham mused. 'There's often a fair amount of "financial irregularity" in schools like this. Which might explain the designer lifestyle.'

Doyle whistled through his teeth. 'You mean he had sticky fingers, sir? With Palmer in on it too? D'you think Kavanagh and Uttley wanted a slice of the action?'

'Could well be. We're going to need to look at the accounts. You can get onto that, Doyle, but for God's sake be discreet. We don't want to put the wind up the governors or anyone else at this stage.'

'What about the students?' asked Burton. 'They'll be in tomorrow. What line do we take with them?'

'Softly-softly for the time being.' Markham paced the length of the stuffy room with the impatience of a man who craved fresh air. 'The school's offering them counselling, so we'll see if that leads anywhere.' He sighed heavily. 'Places like this always have backstory. You need to move a few stones and see what crawls out. Sexual irregularities, sackings, employment tribunals, you know the sort of thing. Murder has a ripple effect, so with any luck we'll get leads from outside the school too.'

'How are we going to divide the interviews, sir?'

Burton was visibly straining at the leash.

'For starters, I'm going to take the heads of department while Noakes works his way through the office staff. I want you to take the older women in the English department, Kate.'

Good call, thought Noakes approvingly. She can have a PC love-in with all the lefties. And bloody good luck with that.

Markham continued, 'We'll both have a crack at Audrey

Burke if Noakes gets nowhere with her, Kate. That woman's hiding something.'

'Like what, sir?'

'Hard to tell, but she looked deathly scared when I saw her outside the LRC. Like a rabbit cornered by a fox. I had the feeling that she'd seen something or knew something.'

Burton snapped her notebook shut. 'What about the head?'

'He's on sick leave. We'll go along with that and keep him on ice for now. The man was certainly in a shocking state, and I don't think we'll get anything coherent out of him just yet.'

Suddenly Markham stopped talking and put a finger to his lips. The message was clear.

Be careful. Walls have ears!

6

Another Body

SUNDAY PASSED WITHOUT ANY breakthrough.

'*Damned with faint praise* just about sums it up,' Markham sighed wearily to Olivia that night as he recounted the events of the day. 'Nobody had a good word to say about poor Ashley. It was all honeyed malice.'

'"The evil that men do lives after them."'

Noting Olivia's tone of reprobation and pity, as well as a certain liquid brightness in her eyes, Markham continued in a mock humorous vein.

'Tracey Roach was especially illuminating.' His lip curled as he reproduced the HR manager's simpering prattle. 'Mr Dean was *very* popular with the secretaries, apparently – *always* dropping by. She had to tell him off because she ran a tight ship and didn't want her team getting distracted. But none of the girls really got a look in, because he was so *wrapped up* in Mr Palmer – the two of them were practically joined at the hip.'

Olivia laughed with her usual bird-like modulation. 'That's Tracey to a tee. I suppose she was gushing like a geyser over Helen Kavanagh.'

'Yes indeed. A case of "The King is dead, long live the King." Kavanagh was lapping up all the salaaming. Talk about a match made in heaven!'

'It's understandable that Tracey was jealous,' Olivia said thoughtfully. 'I mean, she pretty much ruled the roost before he came along. One minute Ashley was mopping the loos, the next he was JP's right-hand man. Knowing Ashley, he probably enjoyed making fun of her to the office staff.'

'Hmm. Well, she looked daggers when she mentioned him dropping by the office, so I reckon you're right about that.'

'But could jealousy have been enough to make her *kill* Ashley, Gil?' Olivia's voice had a solemn cadence, and Markham knew she was seeing that mutilated corpse in her mind's eye.

'I don't know, dearest, I just don't know. Noakes reckons she's more your smiling assassin type, sniping at Ashley from the sidelines.'

Olivia smiled sadly at him. '"Mortals are easily tempted to pinch the life out of their neighbour's buzzing glory, and think that such killing is no murder."'

'Well, whoever gave Ashley that annihilating pinch covered their tracks,' said Markham. 'No forensic clues.'

'Could a woman even have done it?' Olivia sounded incredulous.

'Oh yes.'

Doug 'Dimples' Davidson, the pathologist, had been clear about that. Ashley Dean had been taken by surprise and his jugular slashed prior to mutilation, so the assailant could have been female.

Silence fell. Markham was grateful that Olivia asked nothing about the autopsy. It had been one of the most harrowing that he could remember.

Olivia roused herself to cheerfulness with typically tender concern for her lover's morale.

'Well, who knows, maybe tomorrow will yield something.'

Markham reached for her hand and squeezed it gratefully. 'The students will be back. It'll be useful to see Ashley through their eyes.'

'Some of them really liked him, Gil,' she said softly. 'So, he must have had *some* redeeming features.'

Looking at her candid face, Markham hoped it might be so.

When Monday morning came around, Markham was hard pushed to feel positive. The sea of shrieking students, harsh electric bells and general hubbub constituted an assault on the senses which made him grateful for the sanctuary of his minuscule office. He suspected the rest of the team felt the same way.

Their command post smelt musty and stale but, after a tussle with the grimy window, Doyle eventually succeeded in letting in some fresh air.

As Noakes foraged for tea and biscuits, Markham took stock.

'Anything from the admin crew, Noakes?'

'Pretty much singing from the same hymn sheet as the teachers. Mrs Thing from HR' – there was a soft hiss from Burton – 'gave the impression that some of the dolly birds in the office fancied their chances with Dean but got nowhere cos he was knocking off Palmer.'

'Did she actually *say* that?' Markham enquired heavily, observing that Burton was tight-lipped with disapproval.

'Not in so many words, Guv,' came the cheerful rejoinder. 'But that's what she was driving at. Hinting like mad she was. Very oo-er missus but genteel at the same time, if you know what I mean.'

'Yes, unfortunately I think I do, Sergeant. Mrs Roach practically fell in front of me when I was leaving yesterday so she could shred Ashley's reputation.' Markham paced their temporary cell with knitted brows. 'It was decidedly unedifying.'

The DI wheeled round upon Burton. 'Did you get anything out of the English department, Kate?'

'Well, they avoided innuendo, sir, but they were very close-mouthed. Reading between the lines I'd say Ashley had been trying to get rid of Doctor Abernathy—'

'What did I tell you, Guv?' interjected Noakes through a mouthful of digestive.

'—and the others obviously resented that,' concluded Burton. She broke into a puckish smile which transformed her face. 'I couldn't get Doctor Abernathy to say a bad word about anybody.'

'Could be an act.' It was the voice of experience.

'S'pose so, Sarge.' She sounded reluctant. 'But he wouldn't even join in when they started bitching about Helen Kavanagh. Said being deputy head was a tough call and he thought there was a core of decency ...'

'Sad old duffer.' Noakes shook his head.

The DC returned to her notebook, bent on demonstrating her thoroughness.

'The second in department didn't say much.'

I bet he didn't, the poor sod, thought Markham, recalling scrawny Mike Synott sandwiched between those Beryl Cook lookalikes in the LRC.

Burton rustled her notes. 'There was some talk about Ashley interfering in the department. I haven't quite got my head round all the details,' her brow furrowed, 'but I don't think there's anything which takes us forward in terms of motive.'

Markham breathed a prayer of gratitude that it fell to Burton to decipher the highfalutin gobbledygook which Olivia had warned him was Hope's stock in trade. Noakes had taken one look at the sheaves of *Action Plans*, *Policies* and *Benchmarking Reviews* that Kavanagh had delivered before shoving them unceremoniously into the office's ancient filing cabinet.

'Can't understand a word of it, Guv,' was the DS's verdict. 'This lot are so far up themselves, it's a wonder they can be bothered with the kids at all.'

Right on cue came the sound of scuffling and youthful voices outside the door.

'*You do it!*'

'*No, you!*'

Clearly a few of Hope's student body were about to descend upon them. Suddenly the door burst open, someone having resorted to a hefty shove to resolve the contretemps.

Three teenagers lurched across the threshold. One was a thin, gangly lad whose 'too-cool-for-school' demeanour was undermined by a Stan Laurel hairdo and the fact that his tie appeared to be knotted somewhere under his left ear. The other two were buxom, blowsy young women – one blonde, one brunette (though their natural hair colour was anyone's guess) – who were bursting out of their uniforms and bore a disconcerting resemblance to female wrestlers.

'What can we do for you, guys?' Markham did his best to sound welcoming, however the girls simply stood nudging each other and giggling while the spacey-looking lad stared at the ground.

Burton stepped into the breach.

'Did you want to talk to us about Mr Dean?'

'Yeah,' from the brunette.

Introductions followed. 'I'm Lauren,' she said. 'Me, Nicki and Jake' – jerking a grubby thumb, with chipped peeling nail varnish, at her companions – 'are Student Reps. Mr Uttley said we should be like pupil l … l … l …'

'Liaison,' suggested Burton.

'That's it,' agreed Lauren, nodding gratefully.

Noakes and Doyle stood up and gestured the girls towards their chairs. Spacey Jake remained propped up against the door looking longingly at the digestives. Markham silently handed him the packet and the lad promptly wolfed down four at a speed which had Noakes lost in admiration.

Preliminary courtesies over, Markham prompted the threesome. 'What can you tell us about Mr Dean?'

Lauren was clearly the designated spokesperson.

'Well, he was *dead cool*,' she volunteered. 'Not like a teacher.' Which of course, he wasn't.

Markham nodded encouragingly.

'And he was *dead popular* too. Always called us 'ladies' without being sarky.'

Markham did his best not to display puzzlement at the non-sequitur. He had a feeling that logic was not Lauren's strong suit, but found himself warming to the big untidy girl.

'Didn't half wind our boyfriends up.' No doubt that was the point of the exercise. 'He could be scary if you got on the wrong side of him, though. There was those lads—'

'What about them, Lauren?'

'Well, they got into a fight with Mr Dean innit.'

'What was the fight about?'

'Nobody knew 'zactly. But Mr Dean shouted at them to get out of his office.'

'Mr Dean looked dead upset.' Nicki's voice was the merest whisper. Her pug-like face was distressed. With an almost imperceptible nod, Markham signaled to Noakes to take over the questioning. The DS's coarse tones could become very low and gentle at the right moment.

'D'you have any idea why he was so upset, Nicki?' asked Noakes in a fatherly voice.

The girl's good-natured features turned an unbecoming mauve, leading Markham to suppose that she'd had a king-sized crush on Ashley Dean.

'I heard one of them shouting that he was just a cocky little shit who used to clean the bogs and everyone knew he was Mr Palmer's bumboy.' Classy.

Jake was shuffling his feet. Casually, Noakes drew him into the exchange.

'What's your take on it, Jake? Think we need a bloke's view now.'

No-one can do this quite like Noakesy, thought Markham. Doesn't say much but somehow makes kids feel safe. That's the first time Jake's made eye contact with any of us.

'Yeah, s'right, they was being dead abusive to sir just like Nick said.' Jake's voice gained in confidence. 'And Declan Thompson flipped him the finger on the way out. Everyone saw. They was excluded after that.'

'What did *you* think of Mr Dean?' asked Noakes.

'An OK guy, leastways to me.'

'But not to everyone?'

The boy hesitated and licked dry lips.

'It's all right, lad, anything you say in here is just between us,' reassured Noakes.

'Declan said Mr Dean was bullying his mate Pete Clarke. Said Pete was a ponce and stuff. That's why Dec had a go ...'

Jake fell silent, clearly fearing he had said too much. Once more, his gaze was riveted to the floor.

Markham figured they'd got as much as they were going to get.

'You've been a great help. You can get back off to class now.'

Lauren and Nicki wobbled out on their distinctly non-regulation winkle pickers with Jake bringing up the rear.

'Poor little tykes,' said Noakes as the door shut behind the ill-assorted trio. 'Sounds like Ashley Dean was messing with kids' heads.'

'Maybe the homophobic bullying was an expression of self-disgust, sir,' said Burton earnestly. 'Maybe Ashley was deeply closeted.'

'*Eh?*' Noakes looked mystified, while Doyle's hand was

arrested in mid-air with a biscuit halfway to his mouth.

'Go on,' Markham said.

'It might be that there was some unresolved sexual tension between Ashley and JP which Ashley was exploiting.' Burton was pink with pleasure at having the DI's full attention. 'Or he could've been involved in a full-on affair with JP.'

'Where does the self-hatred come in?' Markham's deep, sonorous voice was interested.

'Well, it's possible Ashley was a straight acting homosexual or bisexual who was ashamed of his gay side. On the other hand, he might not have been homosexual at all – just stringing JP along to further his career. Either way, there might have been an identity crisis and a lot of self-loathing, which would explain his taunting that kid.'

'Or maybe he was just a nasty piece of work who got his jollies winding folk up,' harrumphed Noakes.

Markham weighed the possibilities. 'Ashley certainly played the role of Hope's resident lothario, according to Tracey Roach. But maybe that's all it was – an act – and we should be looking for some sort of infernal triangle.' Noakes's mouth being now so far agape that he resembled a stunned behemoth, Markham clarified, 'A *third wheel*, Sergeant. Someone who was bitterly jealous of the relationship between Ashley and JP.'

Noakes appeared far from convinced, while Doyle simply looked as though this was a long way too deep for him.

The day wore on wearily as they ploughed through the statements of some seventy or so staff with no further interruptions from students. Helen Kavanagh had probably thrown a *cordon sanitaire* around their office, Markham reflected, with a view to controlling the flow of information. Well, he'd break through her defences eventually.

Rubbing his eyes, he glanced at the ugly chrome wall clock. Five fifty-five. The students must be long gone, their stampede for the exit inaudible from this part of the building. He walked to the window. Twilight was falling. The landscape looked chill and colourless, with dun vapour slowly invading the school grounds and making the familiar strange.

Night's black agents to their preys do rouse.

God, he needed to get a grip. Time to roust the senior leadership from wherever they were lurking.

At that moment, there was a soft knock at the door and Tracey Roach slid into the room. Markham wondered how long she had been out there.

'Sorry to interrupt, Officers.' The little girl whisper set the DI's teeth on edge but his keen eyes detected unmistakable anxiety beneath the woman's ingratiating demeanour.

'What is it, Mrs Roach?' He beat back his impatience and strove to sound reassuring.

'It's Audrey Burke, Inspector, I can't seem to find her.'

Markham waved the woman to a chair. 'What do you mean, you can't find her?'

The HR manager anxiously twisted the sleeves of her cardigan. 'I wasn't really listening properly. I think she said she needed to do something ... only she didn't come back.'

Despite the fustiness of the office, Markham suddenly felt icy cold. He recalled the desperate look of entreaty in the face of that pathetic rabbity little woman lurking outside the door of the Learning Resource Centre the previous day. In his mind's eye, he saw her watchful posture, the shifty sidelong glances, the shrinking away from someone just outside his line of vision. *Someone who must have been right there in the LRC.*

I may have signed that woman's death warrant, the DI thought as the clutch of unease tightened its grip. Even though Noakes got nothing out of her initially, I *knew* something wasn't right. I should've warned her she could be putting herself in mortal danger by keeping secrets. Please God let this be a false alarm.

But something told him it wasn't. From the serious looks on the faces of his team, they knew it too.

He forced himself to address Tracey Roach calmly, his lean frame taut as though every molecule in his body had passed through an electric current.

'Think carefully, Mrs Roach, this could be very important. What were her exact words? Did she say she needed to do something or *see someone?*'

Flustered, the woman's eyes darted from Markham to the others and back again.

'I honestly can't say for sure. She was a bit quiet this afternoon, but I didn't think anything of it. Just assumed she was coming down with a cold or something.'

Markham had heard enough. He felt a tingling at his finger ends.

'Right, Noakes, you and Doyle go with Mrs Roach and start checking the building. Jim Snell should be around somewhere, so collect pass keys and whatever else you need from him. Kate, you're with me.'

Tracey Roach looked up at him imploringly. 'I'm sorry, Inspector, I should have realized Audrey was upset and paid more attention.' She spoke without a trace of archness, and Markham liked her all the better for it.

'You're not to blame, Tracey.' The woman blinked at his use of her first name and the gentleness of his voice. 'We all took our eye off the ball. Now, let's get that search started. For all we know, it's nothing sinister and your colleague maybe just needed some time to herself.'

Forty minutes later, Markham and Burton stood in the front courtyard looking up at Hope's bunker-like façade.

There's something deadly about this place, thought Markham. Beneath the chirpy posters and jolly slogans, it's squatting there like a toad. Something evil and misshapen. Something festering in dark corners away from the light. Next to him, Burton shivered as though she felt it too.

The DI's eyes raked the building. And paused.

'What's that?' he asked, pointing to a section of pavement towards the side of the forecourt studded with glass portholes.

Burton frowned then her expression cleared. 'Oh, those are the new music studios. You remember that funny little flight of stairs by the side of the drama theatre, well, that takes you down to the soundproofed practice rooms. The corridor's very narrow and the rooms are just carrels really, so those skylight thingies were the only way to get natural light down there.'

Soundproofed.

'Let's look,' rapped Markham, moving swiftly back towards the school.

Burton panted as she tried to keep up with the DI's long strides. 'It's all secure, sir. There was nobody timetabled to use any of those rooms this afternoon, so Jim Snell locked up around lunchtime.'

'There are any number of duplicate keys in this place, Kate. I saw them all hanging on that rack in Snell's office. He's a lazy bugger, careless too I reckon, so it'd be easy for someone to help themselves. The same someone who was prowling around the night that Ashley Dean's body was discovered.' A note of desperation crept into his voice. 'I hope to God we're not too late.'

Back at the drama theatre, the two detectives stood by the unobtrusive stairwell which led down to the practice rooms. Burton fumbled with her labelled keys under Markham's impatient scrutiny.

'Design and Technology, Expressive Arts, Resistant Materials, Humanities ... Ah, here we are. Music Practice Rooms.'

'Right, we'll be needing your torch, Kate. It looks pretty gloomy down there.'

Burton had her torch out before he had finished speaking and directed a powerful beam down the stairs. Moving almost as one, they descended to the basement where a narrow corridor was lined on one side by four doors with a fifth facing them at the far end. There was no sound save for the rhythmical chug of a generator and the soft hum of one light above the door at the end.

And yet Markham suddenly knew a predator had been there before them. He could *feel* the menace in that submarine-like space with its little cubicles. He badly wanted to be away from it but, in a hoarse voice barely recognizable as his own, gave the instruction, 'Let's check each of these rooms.'

His apprehension had infected Burton who dropped the keys. Time itself seemed to have slowed down, to have contracted to the beating of their hearts in the stuffy airless passage.

Afterwards, Markham retained a vague impression of music stands, instrument cases, stacks of sheet music, and illicit sweet wrappers in the windowless cubby-holes.

All as it should be.

Then they were at the final room. The one at the far end.

'That's the last of them, sir,' exhaled Burton with clear relief as they looked around the bare little studio. 'All clear.'

'No.'

Burton looked at the DI in alarm. The skin seemed stretched over the high cheekbones, and his eyes had a peculiar intensity. Following his gaze, she saw that he was looking at a battered upright Hummel piano with its back next to the wall.

The DC gave a nervous titter. 'Looks like the budget ran out when they got to this one.'

Markham wasn't listening. As though in a trance, he moved across to the Hummel and set his shoulder to the instrument, straining to move it away from the wall. After a second's hesitation, Burton joined him. Flushed and breathing hard, they manoeuvred it into the centre of the tiny room.

Something attracted Burton's attention.

The back of the piano had warped and buckled so that it bulged outwards.

The DC's eyes met Markham's, and a long wordless message passed between them.

With shaking hands, she produced a pen knife from her pocket and inserted the hasp between two of the discoloured sagging panels.

The slight body exploded from the back of the Hummel with a violent crash, the impact of which sounded almost blasphemous in the hieratic stillness of the studio.

Burton's hands went to her mouth as she contemplated the sagging jack-in-the-box that had once been a woman.

Denuded of spectacles, Audrey Burke's milky sightless eyes were rolled back in their sockets. Her lips were drawn back in a rictus of pain and terror. That she had been almost decapitated was evident from a gaping purplish neck wound. Twisted limbs hung at impossible angles, no doubt dislocated as the murderer crammed her pitiful corpse into its makeshift coffin.

Beside him, Burton turned away in horror, but Markham stood motionless.

Nothing could touch Audrey Burke further. All that he could do was call her killer to account. Drinking in every detail of the scene, he noticed an infinitesimally minute shred of paper between the thumb and index finger of the dead woman's right hand. Banknote? A letter? Had she come here with blackmail in mind only to realize too late that she was staring death in the face?

At that moment footsteps pounded above their heads. Noakes and Doyle. Markham squared his shoulders. Two bodies in a little over forty-eight hours. So it begins again, he thought to himself with an ache of despair.

Cloaked by night, the hunter in the shadows watched and waited.

7

Family Snaps

AFTER HOURS OF INTENSE police activity, an uneasy peace finally descended on Hope.

The DI, however, remained on site. He had held it together in front of the team, but now paced up and down his cramped office as though he could somehow out-run the freeze-frames of Audrey Burke's violated corpse which played on an infernal loop in his mind.

Again and again, he saw the crumpled marionette jack-knifing out of its piano frame prison, head lolling grotesquely and scrawny pipe cleaner limbs cruelly wrenched out of position. He dry-heaved as he recalled the slashed throat and hideous fixed grimace. Like some dreadful parody of The Joker from those *Batman* films so beloved by Noakes.

The autopsy would be first thing in the morning. He thought back to the insignificant little woman fingering her drab dirndl skirt, and pictured the flesh hanging from her bones like cold flanks of meat dangling from hooks at the butcher's.

Shuddering, Markham dropped into a chair.

How in God's name would he break it to Olivia? He felt guilty that he had not phoned her, merely texting to say that there had been a development. Audrey's death would wring her heart. Better that she should take her rest.

He shut his eyes, but the gruesome images seared his eyeballs. Morbidly he wondered how the undertakers would make those pitiful remains acceptable for viewing by the family. Would they sew the head back on as they did for victims of the guillotine in days gone by? Could their formaldehyde and fillers convert that awful death-snarl into a smile? He felt unutterably sad as he thought of Audrey Burke's final makeover.

Markham started up from the chair and went towards the window, momentarily forgetting where he was, his hands clenching and unclenching as he stared unseeing into the darkness.

There was no escaping the fact that he had been a negligent fool. He had failed Audrey. Hadn't looked beyond the mousy exterior to the vulnerable woman beyond. Hadn't followed up his intuition that she was badly scared of someone at Hope. Hadn't tried to win her confidence or warn her that she could be at risk. He had ignored what was staring him in the face. As he imagined the PA's terror when her executioner dropped his mask and she realized that this was the end, he wondered if he would ever be able to forgive himself.

'Guv.'

Markham was jerked from his gloomy reflections by

Noakes. He glanced at the wall clock and saw that it was 2 a.m.

'What're you doing here, Noakes? Your shift doesn't start for several hours.'

Noakes scratched his head awkwardly. 'Figured you could do with some company, boss. I'll get a brew on.'

The DS's gruff solicitude touched Markham. For the first time in several hours he felt a sense of purpose.

'Sleep well, Audrey,' he whispered as Noakes hovered at the fridge. 'We'll get the bastard, never fear.'

'What's that, boss?' Noakes eyed the DI warily as though he suspected him of climbing the walls.

'Nothing Noakesy. Just talking to myself.'

Noakes padded across the room with a steaming cup, his resemblance to a St Bernard dog more pronounced than ever. After the horrors of the night, his stolidity and dumb sympathy put new heart into Markham.

'There you go, Guv. No toast till the canteen opens.' At these blessedly normal words and the comforting warmth of the tea, Markham slowly felt the icy hand of death release its clutch.

The two men sat companionably. Eventually Noakes broke the silence.

'Sorry I didn't get Audrey to open up, Guv. I gave it my best shot but reckon the poor cow must've made her own plans.'

'That's all right.' Markham regarded the DS steadily. 'She was obviously petrified of someone and I should've kept a closer eye on her, gone in harder, begged her not to go it alone ...'

Markham's voice trailed off miserably.

'Don't beat yourself up, Guv. She was nuts about Palmer, wasn't she?'

'Yes, Olivia said she'd been making puppy-dog eyes at him for years. Thought the sun rose and set on him.'

'Should've gone to Specsavers.' Noakes broke into a grin, then coughed apologetically and went on with his theory. 'If she was trying to protect Palmer, then maybe she thought she could strike a deal. Olivia said Ashley was nasty about Audrey. Called her gormless or some such?' Markham nodded confirmation. 'Well, that could've made her sympathize with the killer – prepared to keep shtum provided the head was safe.'

'You could be right, Noakes. I think Audrey was on to something. Whatever the secret was, she paid for it with her life. If only I could have warned her she was playing with fire!'

'She'd probably have gone ahead anyway, Guv. My Muriel...,' Here Markham braced himself for second-hand psychological insights of doubtful provenance. 'Well, she says that some women of that age go all fuzzy ... you know, get mad ideas about blokes and things.'

From what Markham recalled of Mrs Noakes, he reckoned there was little chance of her 'too solid flesh' succumbing to fuzziness but, as ever, his DC's pronouncements contained a nugget of common sense.

'Yes, Noakes,' he conceded wryly, 'it's quite possible that where JP was concerned, Audrey wasn't rational. Erotomania or De Clerambault's syndrome or some combination of the two.'

'*Eh?*'

The DI hastily returned to the vernacular. 'She'd likely

have clammed up if I applied the thumbscrews. But I wish to God I'd at least tried.'

'Burton said when you found her she had a bit of paper in her right hand.' Noakes was keen to jolt Markham out of further introspection.

'Yes, it looked like a banknote, though we'll need forensics to confirm.' The DI's fingers drummed an impatient tattoo. 'Was this blackmail?'

'Yeah, Guv. Money could've changed hands, then the killer wrenched it out of her hand when he was stuffing her into the back of the piano.'

Markham was thoughtful. 'That sounds feasible, Noakes. But what puzzles me is why she agreed to meet him on her own in the music practice rooms. Even allowing for the fact that she wasn't thinking straight, that was a terrible gamble.'

'He must have been very reassuring.' Noakes spoke with conviction. 'Made her believe she was safe with him. An' maybe she figured some of the kids would be around – jamming or summat.'

'Yes, our man – or woman – was able to lull Audrey into a false sense of security. Plausible. Smooth-talking. Outwardly harmless. In reality, subtle, calculating and dangerous.'

Noakes eventually lumbered off home, assured by the DI that he would not be long following.

But still he sat there, light-headed with fatigue, as though there was a spell upon him, keeping him motionless, while terrible images were imprisoned within his eyes.

2.55.

All existence seemed to beat with a lower pulse than his own ...

Just then, Markham's eye fell on a pair of grubby trainers wedged behind the filing cabinet and inspiration struck.

Rather than go home and wake up Olivia, or pull an all-nighter at Hope, he would drop by 'Doggie' Dickerson's Gym in Marsh Lane where Bromgrove Police Boxing Club had its unofficial headquarters. Like a vampire, Doggie never seemed to sleep and was invariably to be found in his dingy little office, a bottle of the strong stuff to hand and a tale to suit every ear. Markham guessed the antecedents of some of his sparring partners wouldn't bear close inspection, but he found Doggie's fetid den, with its heaving, grunting inmates, oddly soothing. For the fellowship, he supposed. And the chance to go ten rounds with DCI Sidney by proxy. Yes, if Doggie could accommodate him, nothing would revive him like imagining that he was knocking seven bells out of Slimy Sid!

Having locked up behind him, Markham set the alarm as Jim Snell had shown him then stood outside in the fore-court looking back at the school. Wreathed in mist, it seemed almost to be vanishing from sight like *The Flying Dutchman* or some other ghost ship.

With one last look, the DI turned his back on it and walked towards the car park.

Some thirty minutes later, drenched in sweat and breathing heavily, Markham felt like a man reborn.

Arriving at the gym, he had found cocky Chris Carstairs, a young DI from Vice doing squat thrusts in a corner while a couple of local undesirables were slogging it out in one of the three rings. Such was the mysterious freemasonry of Doggie's, that distinctions of rank ceased to matter. All that counted was pushing oneself to the limit and measuring one's strength alongside other men.

"'Lo, Gil. Haven't seen you round here for a bit,' sang out Carstairs on spotting him. 'You must be out of practice,' he declared, eyeing Markham's anatomy as though minutely choosing his point of attack. 'Fancy your chances against me? I'll pull my punches, I promise!'

A guffaw floated out of Doggie's office at this feeble witticism. Then the proprietor himself shambled out, looking as disreputable as ever, his straggly grey hair, nicotine stained fingers and yellow tombstone teeth distinctly at odds with the complacent look he bestowed on his little kingdom.

'Morning, Inspector,' he rasped. 'Good to see you. This 'ere young fella's on at me to give 'im a workout, so reckon you could help me out.'

The 'workout' wiped the smirk off Carstairs' face, so business-like and bloodthirsty was the way in which he was demolished despite landing some heavy punches. Markham himself was surprised by the reserves of energy which seemed to have come to his aid out of nowhere. Despite lack of sleep, it was as if he had drunk a great draught of fury and indignation which insulated him from his colleague's bull-like proceedings. *That was for Audrey. And that, and that*! Then, when Carstairs got to his feet and squared up once again, the faceless murderer gave way to DCI Sidney. *Take that, you bastard. And that*!

'Whoa!' Doggie was finally aroused to something almost approaching animation as the other went down once again. "'E's not looking too pretty, Mr Markham. I'd say you've won.'

From a prone position, Carstairs eyed him with dazed

respect before allowing himself to be helped down from the ring.

'That was too many for me, Gil,' he observed before adding suspiciously, 'have you been training somewhere else on the sly? I've never seen you like that before. You'd be a useful light heavyweight for the Federation Cup team, mate. I could put in a word if you like.'

'I'm flattered, Chris.' And it was true, he *did* feel a savage exultation in his victory. 'But I lack your dedication.' He clapped the other man on the shoulder and said warmly, 'Any time you feel like a grudge match, though ...'

Carstairs grinned ruefully. 'I'm not likely to underestimate you again, Gil.'

Doggie having retreated to his lair, the two men lingered companionably next to the ring, idly watching the other match in progress.

'You're on the Hope Academy case, Gil?'

'That's right.' Markham exhaled slowly, not choosing to say more. Carstairs was unperturbed by his curtness. Doggie's was a last bastion against the horrors of the job, and officers rarely talked shop there.

'Kids from Hope went on the rampage in the town centre last Christmas,' he murmured, before adding with a sideways glance at Markham, 'it's a tough gig being a teacher there.'

'Hmm,' Markham grunted non-committally.

'There's been the odd scandal too ... teachers getting too friendly with pupils, that kind of thing.' Carstairs wrinkled his brows upwards as if teased by a fleeting memory. 'And a few years back the head had to retire in a hurry ... All hushed up of course. Fingers in the till, as I remember it.'

Sex and money spinning their endless webs. Wasn't it always the way, thought Markham. Somehow, he had to unravel the threads and find that gossamer-fine connection with Ashley Dean and Audrey Burke.

'Right, Gil, as you've had the bad taste to thrash me, I'm off. Let me know if you change your mind about the squad.' Carstairs chuckled. 'You can bring Noakes along as your second. He c'n drink your share of the beer.'

'A match made in heaven,' came the dry rejoinder as Markham toweled himself off. He decided to have a shower at the station rather than take the risk of contracting something unspeakable from Doggie's facilities. Noakes would be in before long, and they could plan the day ahead.

Later that morning, having returned to Hope, Markham and Noakes got into their car, a standard issue Ford Fiesta from the station pool which was hardly likely to enhance their kudos with the little knot of teenagers loitering about the front courtyard making an elaborate pretence of disinterest in the police comings and goings. Out of respect for Audrey Burke, the school was closed to students though lessons would resume the following day. Markham noted with sadness that tributes to her were conspicuous by their absence from the forecourt.

Markham had decided to leave Doyle and Burton at the school with Forensics while he and Noakes went to check up on James Palmer. For all the DS's shortcomings, Markham found his dishevelled companion a curiously comforting presence even now when, as designated chauffeur, he was grinding gears with the ferocity of a Formula One driver.

James Palmer lived in Calderstones Drive, a highly

sought-after address in a leafy suburb of Bromgrove, about twenty-five minutes away from the school. Strangely enough, even though a cold wind was gusting and no leaves were rustling on the mighty oaks which reared ominously above them, Markham felt more at ease with Bromgrove's chill melancholy than the stifling oppression of Hope and its Stalin-esque surveillance. Perhaps it was different for kids today, he reflected, but that soulless bunker made him nostalgic for the cosy shabbiness which had been the setting for most of his own schooldays.

But it wasn't just that, he thought, trying to pin down the source of his disquiet. Parapsychologists and exorcists talked of a 'cold spot' in haunted buildings, didn't they? Well, he'd felt something similar at Hope this morning, for all the raucous din of a sprawling school community. There had been a sense of malevolence so strong that it was like a presence at his shoulder, as though the spirit of Evil was breathing softly down the back of his neck. And yet, he could not grasp this shadowy spectre nor hold it fast.

'Nearly there, Guv,' grunted Noakes, recalling Markham with a jolt to the present. 'How d'you want to play the interview with Palmer?'

'Low key. We won't even call it an interview. More a friendly house call to see how he's coping with the trauma blah-de-blah. How's your bedside manner, Noakes?' He regarded his subordinate with a quizzical expression. 'No need to answer that!'

Noakes turned into a quiet cul-de-sac lined with detached and terraced Victorian period houses.

'Right, here we are. Number 4 Calderstones Drive. Cushty!

He's done all right for himself!'

Markham considered the impressive semi-detached property thoughtfully. Spread over four storeys, it oozed exclusivity and looked to have around half an acre of manicured lawn to the sides and rear.

'Indeed he has, Sergeant!' The DI figured they were looking at a cool half a million's worth of prime real estate.

'I thought he was divorced with kids at uni.' Noakes was puzzled. 'How's he managed to hang on to this lot?'

Markham wondered how he could have afforded it in the first place, even on a headmaster's salary.

'Separated, not divorced, Noakes. But you're right, I can't imagine he'll be keeping it if there's a divorce in the offing.'

Noakes climbed shallow sandstone steps to the elegantly porticoed front door followed by Markham.

The DS's hand was raised to the solid brass bell push when the 'character' front door, complete with stained-glass antique panels, swung open to reveal a blonde pocket Venus attired in chinos and a cashmere sweater. A heady blast of Chanel No. 5 knocked both officers backwards, so that they were momentarily disorientated.

Markham was the first to recover.

'Mrs Palmer?'

'For my sins.' It was a low, husky voice, not unattractive. 'You'll be the police. Come in.'

The high-ceilinged, light-filled hallway had tasteful checkerboard marble tiling in black and white. A chunky mahogany jardinière stand was the only furniture, and Markham admired the elegant restraint which had preserved the heritage feel of the property.

The two men were led into a surprisingly cosy, sash-windowed living room and ushered to a moss-green Chesterfield. As he made the introductions, Markham briefly took in the elegant but comfortable mix of antique and modern furniture, William Morris wallpaper and nineteenth-century botanical prints before concentrating his attention on Cheryl Palmer. Sporting a silver-frosted Farrah Fawcett hairstyle of the sort favoured by the Duchess of Cornwall, she had a delicate heart-shaped face whose smoothness spoke of an expensive beauty regime. A silver-framed photograph on the adjacent side-table showed a younger leggy replica, with long tortoise-shell tresses and the same gamine features.

'That's Jemima, our youngest,' Cheryl said, following Markham's gaze. Her voice was proud. 'She's in her first year at Durham.'

Breaking off, as though her mind was elsewhere, their hostess offered them tea or coffee. The DI interposed smoothly before Noakes could accept.

'We don't propose to take up too much of your time, Mrs Palmer. Just wanted to see how your husband's bearing up. We know Mr Dean was his protégé and he'd done a great deal to bring him on.'

Markham said nothing of the second murder.

Cheryl's lips trembled as she fought for composure. 'That place sucked the life out of him. He had nothing left for me and the kids. That's why we separated. Not cos there were three of us in the bloody marriage or anything like that, but on account of Hope taking up all his energy. And now he just sits chain smoking, moaning to himself and rocking backwards and forwards. Like he's lost his mind.'

She appeared oblivious to the possibility of her soon-to-be ex-husband having turned to a *man* for comfort. Was her unconcern genuine or simulated, Markham wondered.

Markham groped for the right words. 'I know this will seem poor comfort to you now, Mrs Palmer, but time is a great healer. With proper support, hopefully your husband can come to terms with what's happened.'

The woman's mouth twisted. 'He won't ever get better till he's out of there, Inspector. It was just one crisis after another. He got no peace.'

'What sort of thing d'you mean, luv?' Noakes enquired innocently.

'Oh, it was all sorts. The business of that maths teacher ... then before that, some woman in the English department. A nymphomaniac redhead ...'

Noakes winked suggestively. 'Teachers getting it on in the stationery cupboard, were they?'

Markham found he was holding his breath.

'Nothing like that. The silly bint got involved with a sixth-former. Lots of *special tuition* before the parents kicked up a stink. Everyone was buzzing about it. They were quite brazen – seen out together after he left, apparently. Various governors were up in arms. The whole saga gave James an ulcer.' The beautifully shaped brows puckered. 'Hey, come to think of it, I think she was the one caught up in that awful business at St Mary's.' Cheryl made a moue of distaste. 'There's always a drama with some women.' It sounded to Markham like a mocking echo of DCI Sidney.

The DI's heart was palpitating violently. He felt as though poisoned weapons had been hurled at him. The pain of the sting was almost unbearable. His recent bruising encounter in the ring was nothing to it.

Why had Olivia never told him about this? What else had she kept hidden?

Seeing that the guv'nor was dangerously poised, Noakes came to the rescue.

'If you remember, sir, we've got that appointment on the other side of town.'

Somehow Markham found his voice.

'Of course, Sergeant. Mrs Palmer, we don't want to disturb your husband while he is resting. But please pass on our best wishes for his recovery. No, don't trouble yourself, we'll see ourselves out.'

Afterwards, Markham could not remember how he had got out of the house. He only knew that he needed to see Olivia as soon as possible.

8

Clearing The Air

BY AN UNSPOKEN TELEPATHY, the two officers did not speak until they were well away from Calderstones Drive.

'Where to, Guv?' Noakes eventually enquired, eyeing Markham warily. He could see from the tight set of the DI's mouth that his guvnor was upset.

Markham did not immediately reply. Misgivings assailed him like a regiment of furies beating at the walls of his brain. The view outside the car windows mirrored his mood, grass and trees setting up a dull shiver under late morning clouds that hid the sun fitfully.

Why hadn't Olivia been completely frank? Why hadn't she told him about this ... this business with a student? And why the hell had she left him to find it out from the headmaster's wife of all people!

Markham made no reply, and Noakes, realizing that the guv'nor was in no mood for repartee, took refuge in his own thoughts.

For a moment, back there in Palmer's house, Noakes had thought Markham was going to keel over; his face had turned a funny putty colour and when they came out, his knuckles gripping the car handle had been white. He was willing to bet all the guv'nor could think about now was clearing the air with his girlfriend. Personally, he couldn't imagine Olivia doing anything dodgy, but the guv'nor had her on a pedestal. Hearing Cheryl Palmer's gossip had been ... well ... like seeing a crack appear in crystal. Noakes blinked in surprise at himself. There was something about Olivia Mullen which made him come over all poetical!

'Drop me at home, will you, Noakes.' The words were abrupt and awkward. 'There're ... one or two things I need to attend to ...'

'Right you are, Guv.' Noakes's face was impassive. Smoothly, he pointed the car towards The Sweepstakes.

Markham found Olivia sitting curled up in her favourite armchair, staring dreamily into space. A book, open but clearly unread, lay in her lap. Her face lit up at his entrance.

'*Gil! How I've missed you!*' she cried, and then seeing the shock in her lover's face, she said, 'What is it, Gil?'

For the first time in their relationship, she had the sense of a chill fog having gathered between them – of them somehow missing each other's mental track.

'Noakes and I called on Cheryl Palmer today, Liv.' Markham's deep baritone was hoarse.

The candid eyes regarded him expectantly.

'You didn't tell me there'd been an,' he stumbled over his words, 'an incident with a sixth former.'

The words felt like pincers, but somehow he got them out.

Olivia looked at him incredulously.

'What on earth are you talking about?'

Then the mist cleared. She sprang up from her chair, the unread book falling to the floor.

'Ah, now I see it!' she cried. 'An incident with a sixth former!' Her face was hard and set – something quite new in Markham's experience of her – with a rigid animosity that made him recoil with a sensation close to fear.

'I—'

'You're saying that I had an affair with a schoolboy. Well, what if I did? It's none of your business. Are you now going to pry into my early life? I don't suppose your life story is all good clean fun! You think—'

The hot blood rushed to her face before receding, leaving her deathly pale.

Markham felt wretchedly jarred. 'In God's name, Liv, what's got into you? I never said—'

'I suppose that bitch Cheryl set out to make mischief, and you believed all that she told you! Well, if you want to take the word of a malicious trouble-maker whose marriage has broken down, that's your privilege. You can believe what you like.'

Olivia's words were like the cut of a lash, her eyes dangerously bright as though lit by vindictive fire. She was in the grip of a rebellious anger that Markham had never seen before, almost as though she was reliving some long-buried scene from her past, from before he knew her. Had this happened before in another time and place? What other secrets had she kept from him? He felt a new rush of gall and wheeled round to the other side of the room, his mind struggling to take in these new impressions.

Pain rippled across Olivia's face like the shadow of a sob. 'Right,' she cried, 'I'll leave you to your mean-minded speculation. Much good may it do you!'

Eluding his outstretched arm, she flung out of the room and the next minute he heard the key turn in their bedroom door.

Markham sank into the chair she had vacated, feeling with a clutch of despair at his heart that he had handled the whole scene disastrously. The faint scent of Olivia's perfume only increased his torment.

He must have been sitting there a full quarter of an hour staring blankly before him when he heard Olivia emerge.

Moving swiftly into the hallway, he found her wrapped up in coat and scarf, a bulging tote bag on her shoulder.

'Where are you going, Liv?'

'It's none of your business. You don't own me.'

Something in his stricken face must have touched a chord.

'I'm going to stay with Wendy for a bit. You and I ... need a break from each other.'

Markham felt that he had too much to bear that day and his head fell.

When he looked up again, she was gone.

The door had barely closed behind Olivia when Markham's mobile rang. It was Noakes with news that there had been a development.

Looking sadly round the apartment, which seemed already to bear a lonelier aspect, he instructed the DS to send a driver because his own car was at the station.

Then he steeled himself to return to the fray.

Hope was eerily quiet when Markham reached it some thirty minutes later. No sign of pupils, though it was not yet going-home time.

'They've given the kids the afternoon for Enrichment,' Noakes told him.

Yet more educational patois. 'What's that when it's at home, Sergeant?'

Noakes grinned sheepishly. 'Just means they've bussed 'em off to the Hoxton Sports Centre for extra PE.'

'Good.' Markham savoured the unexpected calm. 'The more time they spend off-site the better right now.'

Burton looked up from a pile of paperwork. 'It's half term next week, sir, so they're winding down anyway.'

Noakes scanned Markham's face for any clue as to how it had gone with Olivia. The DI had his usual air of self-possession but, on closer observation, looked wiped out.

Markham slumped into the nearest chair and stared moodily across at the window, running a hand through his thick dark hair and trying to ignore the bitter, incessant murmur within him. *Olivia, Olivia.*

The DS read the runes. Trouble at Mill.

They've had a fight, he thought. An' no making-up neither from the look on the guv'nor's face.

Obscurely bothered, Noakes abandoned his half-finished bag of cheesy Wotsits, debating with himself how he could best discover the lie of the land. Something about the set of Markham's mouth suggested that any enquiries were likely to be repelled.

Outside, blustery rain was still coming down in sheets, the bushes outside twisting and flailing violently as though in the grip of Saint Vitus Dance.

Suddenly Markham was jolted out of his lethargy. '*What the hell*!'

'What is it, sir?' Burton sprang to attention.

Markham was at the window in three swift strides.

Nothing.

'I could have sworn there was someone out there just now. Watching us.'

'Not when it's pissing down!' said Noakes, 'That's *Hound of the Baskervilles*, Guv!'

The DI forced a smile. The glimpse of hate-filled eyes locking onto his and lips contorted in a snarl was so fleeting that he could not be sure he hadn't imagined it – hadn't somehow conjured up the image of a voyeur, a shadow man stalking them from the sidelines, a fox watching the hunters. Yet he couldn't shake the conviction that the killer was close at hand, adapting his steps to theirs with the stealthy precision of a subtly constructed reflex machine. He blanched at the thought, but then noticed Burton's anxious scrutiny. Better pull himself together or the DC would go all mother-hen on him. With consciousness of the earlier scene still sharp within him, he writhed under the idea of anyone pitying him.

The DS narrowed his eyes at Burton's solicitous expression. What *was* it about the boss that made women come over all unnecessary? The silly cow was looking at Markham as if he'd come down from heaven. From the sly grin on Doyle's face, he figured the lad had noticed it too.

Noakes was the unlikeliest of troubadours and could never have explained what it was about Olivia Mullen which compelled his tongue-tied devotion. *She's good for the guv'nor*, was as far as his reasoning ever took him. But one thing was for sure. He wasn't going to let some snot-nosed DC get between the boss and his girlfriend. If Burton needed setting straight, then *he* was the man to do it.

The DI was looking at him expectantly. Putting thoughts of knight-errantry to one side, Noakes hastened to update him.

'A letter's turned up, Guv. Looks like it was written by JP to Ashley. Typed, no signature, but it's obvious that's who it's from.' Noakes cleared his throat uncomfortably.

'Come on, man, spit it out.' Markham was peremptory.

'Well ...' The DS looked hopefully at Burton and Doyle but neither of them came to his aid. 'It was very lovey-dovey, Guv.' Noakes blushed and appeared fascinated by his stubby finger tips.

'I see,' Markham replied patiently. 'Explicit? Pornographic?'

Noakes turned a deeper shade of magenta, now fiddling with the buttons of his none-too-fresh shirt.

'Nowt like that, Guv. Just said how much he, er, cared for Ashley an' all about what he'd done for him ... proper soppy till the end—'

'That's when he threatened to kill himself and Ashley too.' Burton decided it was time to cut to the chase.

Noakes drew himself up and shot her a withering look.

'I was just coming to that bit,' he said huffily. 'He said if Ashley ever two-timed him, he'd do for them both.'

Markham held out his hand.

'Let's see it then.'

'Ms Kavanagh's got it, Guv,' piped up Doyle.

Markham stared at them.

'Why?' His tone was several degrees below zero.

Noakes offered a deprecating smile. 'The caretaker brought it to the Forensics lads earlier today. Said he found it when he was checking Ashley's locker. We were looking at it when the Kavanagh crone swooped by on her broomstick.'

'She said she needed to see if there were any implications from an HR point of view.'

Burton's voice trailed off in the face of Markham's stony displeasure, thunder and lightning gathering about his brow and eyes.

Bloody Kavanagh. And bloody Jim Snell. That locker should have been checked at the outset.

'Right, Noakes, let's pay Ms Kavanagh a visit, shall we?'

The other two did their best to look invisible as the DI stalked off with Noakes at his heels, but once the door had slammed behind them, Doyle let out a long whistle.

'Phew, that was a close call! I wonder what's eating him.'

Burton glanced at him repressively, but the young PC simply flashed her a good-natured grin, rumpling his ginger quiff until it stood on end like the quills of a porcupine.

'Oh c'mon, Kate, lighten up. The guvnor looked like death warmed up. And if looks could kill ...' He winked expressively. 'Trouble on the domestic front, I reckon.'

'We don't know that.' Burton's voice was cold.

'Got to be. She's older than him. Cloughie in Traffic saw them together the other day. He said—'

'Aren't you supposed to be checking out Hope's finances?' Despite an almost painful hunger to hear more about the woman who had stolen Markham's heart, the DC was brisk.

Doyle rolled his eyes. 'All right, all right, you win! I'm on it.' Reluctantly, he turned his attention to the sheaf of papers in front of him.

A wistful shadow fell across Kate Burton's face. Suppressing a sigh, she resumed her perusal of staff witness statements.

There was something up with the thermostat in Helen Kavanagh's office. The room felt like a sauna, Markham thought irritably, as he registered the toasty ambience. As his feet sank into the thick pile of an expensive-looking aquamarine carpet and he noted the deputy head's top-of-the-range workstation and country-house overstuffed armchairs, he felt more convinced than ever that Kavanagh had been feathering her own nest to the detriment of the school. While the staffroom possessed all the allure of a dilapidated rest home for the terminally bewildered, *her* quarters resembled a five-star hotel penthouse. No doubt Tracey Roach and the other serfs were detailed to provide room service on tap.

'Welcome to my home from home, Inspector!' Kavanagh cooed. Almost as if she had been able to read his thoughts, she added pointedly, 'I would have settled for something utilitarian and no-frills, of course, but the *dear* governors wouldn't hear of it. They positively *insisted* it should be nothing but the best for Hope's officer corps!'

Markham was willing to bet Kavanagh hadn't put up much resistance. No way was *she* going to slum it with the rank and file.

With a sudden pang, Markham recalled Olivia's withering commentary. 'Kavanagh's *such* a champagne socialist!' she had scoffed, her eyes emitting sparks. '*All animals are equal, but some are more equal than others.* JP's another lord of the swill-bucket. Snouts in the trough, the pair of them!'

What if he had lost Olivia forever? The thought rushed through him in an agony of terror.

A polite cough recalled him to his surroundings.

Harry Mountfield came forward diffidently to meet him.

'Harry's the Staff Wellbeing Rep.'

Mountfield somehow managed not to look ironic. Markham and Noakes regarded him with sympathy as they were ushered towards three armchairs so vast and chintzy that they looked like giant anemones from a David Attenborough nature documentary.

'I wondered if Harry could shed some light on JP's ...' Kavanagh heaved a theatrical sigh, *'inner torment.'* She swivelled to fix Mountfield with her beady, porcine gaze. Clearly, Palmer's meltdown, along with the whiff of scandal about him, offered a boost to the deputy head's own career prospects.

The head of religious studies looked somewhat askance at the deputy head's penny dreadful mode of proceeding.

'I think there *was* some special feeling between JP and Ashley,' he said quietly. 'You could see it in the way they looked at each other.' A spasm of emotion – pity? disgust? – crossed his bluff features.

'Might he have been jealous of Ashley's affection for someone else? Jealous enough to kill?' Markham asked tentatively.

Mountfield looked troubled. 'Who can say what any of us is capable of, Inspector?' He hesitated, visibly wrestling with himself. 'If you're asking me *could* JP have done it, then the answer's yes. If you're asking me *did* he do it ...' He threw up his arms helplessly. 'And now Audrey ...'

I am in blood stepped in so far that, should I wade no more, returning were as tedious as go o'er.

Markham heard Olivia's clear, sweet voice in his inner ear. God, the pain was like a knife in his guts.

Back to the present and Helen Kavanagh, who was brandishing two sheets of typescript at him. Silently, he absorbed their contents before handing them to Noakes.

'It doesn't follow that Mr Palmer actually wrote the letter. If indeed it was a letter,' he said.

'But who ... why...?' Kavanagh did a passable impression of bewilderment, though Markham was sure she had already worked it out.

'It would be easy enough for anyone who'd watched Ashley and the head together – stalked them, even – to produce such an account and then plant it in Ashley's locker to which,' here Markham shot a baleful glance at Noakes, 'every Tom, Dick and Harry potentially had access. Jim Snell has a master set of locker keys, all labelled, so a thief could have done the business in minutes.' Ignoring Kavanagh's look of consternation, the DI continued remorselessly. 'Or it might be that Mr Palmer confided his thoughts to paper as a private exercise – never intending Ashley to see what he had written – only for someone to use it after the murder to frame him.'

'That's a powerful hatred,' murmured Mountfield.

'Or love,' countered the DI. 'Two sides of the same coin, remember.'

The teacher turned his eyes on Markham with a melancholy, almost reproachful look quite at odds with his normal merry demeanour. Recalling that Mountfield was Olivia's

120

friend, Markham felt sadly as though he was hurting her anew.

Before Kavanagh had time to recover her equilibrium, Markham said firmly, 'We'll be speaking to Mr Palmer just as soon as he's fit to be interviewed. In the meantime, I would ask you to keep this confidential.' Some hope.

Out in the corridor, the DI instructed Noakes, 'Chase up Doyle and the accounts. I've a hunch Kavanagh and maybe one or two others may have been lining their own pockets.'

'D'you think this is about money, Guv?'

Markham shook his head. 'No, Sergeant, I think it's something so twisted and warped that God knows where it will take us.' He felt sure, with an insistent sense of foreboding pressing down on him like an iron bar, that these murders did not spring from mammon. No, it was more the voice of Moloch that he heard hissing sibilantly in his ear. *Vengeance is mine, I shall repay.* But Vengeance against whom and for what?

As Noakes's stocky form receded down the corridor, Markham was hit by a wave of exhaustion so strong that he reeled against the wall.

God, they were up against it with this case and no mistake. The team needed a break before the vultures of the press began circling in earnest. He shuddered at the thought of the lurid headlines. *Top cop outed as lover of sexy suspect in school slayings.* The fact that Olivia hadn't even been on the premises at the time of Audrey's murder would no doubt be conveniently overlooked in the quest for a juicy backstory. If that happened, DCI Sidney would jump all over them. They might as well forget nailing the killer and getting justice for the victims. Slimy Sid would join the conga behind Helen Kavanagh, Hope's governors and Bromgrove LEA to ensure that neither the town's flagship academy nor its police force was tarnished by any inconvenient scandals.

'Ten to one, they'll try to pin it on some local nutter, just like Kavanagh suggested,' he muttered.

Again, the exhaustion hit him. He felt like a somnambulist, but there was no point going back to the Sweepstakes for some shut-eye. He couldn't bear the thought of the apartment without Olivia.

Listlessly, he wondered what she would tell Wendy about their quarrel. Of course, her friend would take Olivia's side and regard him as a shit of the first water.

But, dammit, he hadn't been such a brute, had he? What was he supposed to think when Cheryl Palmer sprang that story on him? He had thought there were no secrets between himself and Olivia, but she hadn't thought it worth her while to share those details of her personal history with him despite roaming far and wide on other aspects of Hope.

Suddenly the voice of conscience seemed to whisper in his ear.

Olivia's implicit trust in the integrity of her own behaviour, together with her faith in him, was such that she could never have anticipated his jealous reaction.

Jealousy. For that is what it was. The thought of his lover having ever been involved with another man was like imagining that someone else had breathed on the crystal that he wanted to keep untouched and unclouded.

By what right had he challenged her behaviour when she had never probed *his* past – had never attempted to unseal the trauma that he carried from his abusive childhood?

Self-disgust surged like venom through his system. What wouldn't he give to speak to her now. The scene in their apartment would have a very different ending.

Markham began to pace up and down the corridor with the restlessness of a wild animal that sensed its prey near at hand.

The killer was close by, he could *feel* it.

Unless he moved quickly, tragedy would strike again!

9

Fear and Loathing

THE CAR PARK OF Our Lady of the Angels was overflowing
when Noakes and Markham arrived the following morning
for the Requiem Mass of Ashley Dean.

As Noakes carefully manoeuvred their car into the last
available space, Markham examined the small gothic church.
Situated at the end of Chilcot Avenue, just a few roads away
from Hope, it was an unpretentious squat building of sandstone blackened in places with damp. Markham vaguely
recalled hearing that it was deemed to be a fine example
of Victorian gothic, but there were no flying buttresses or
soaring spires here, just a modestly gabled slate roof and bell
tower atop bulging walls which seemed to huddle together for
warmth as though wracked by rheumatism. This impression
of stoical misery was heightened by the miserable weather,
sheets of rain lashing the building which crouched mutely
before the storm.

To one side of the church was a two-storeyed stone house,

also in red sandstone, which Markham took to be the presbytery. On the other was a Calvary; he noticed Noakes giving it furtive glances out of the corner of his eye, as though the DS had a superstitious terror of being struck down for irreligious thoughts.

Noakes had clearly put some thought into his choice of attire. Markham presumed it was his Sunday best, though it gave him the unfortunate appearance of a retired mobster. Markham felt a needle-sharp stab of pain at the thought of how much he would have enjoyed Olivia's gentle ribbing on the subject.

Of course, she would be there – was probably already inside with her colleagues from Hope. Would she acknowledge him? Or would she shrink away with revulsion? He could bear anything but that, he told himself, feeling wretched at the thought that he had committed the worst kind of sacrilege – that of tearing down the altar of trust which was the bedrock of their relationship.

Noakes was wriggling uncomfortably, eyeing his surroundings with unmistakable apprehension. Markham supposed it was the physical equivalent of shouting 'No Popery' at the top of his voice.

'Right, Sergeant, better get in there,' he said resignedly. 'Just follow my lead if you're not sure about all the bobbing and genuflecting.'

The DS, looking anything but reassured, reached for the car door handle.

When they walked into the church, the cloying scent of lilies was so strong that it almost knocked Markham backwards. They were everywhere – great banks of them – so that

Markham barely noticed the marble sanctuary and reredos, side chapels and myriad plaster statues of saints whose mouths were well turned down at the corners as though they shared the general melancholy.

At the front of the sanctuary, next to trestles which awaited the coffin, was a massive stainless steel framed picture of Ashley Dean in his golden, glowing prime, posing with his surf board on some foreign beach. High above the sanctuary, hail rattled like shot against stained glass windows featuring yet more saints in ruby and turquoise robes. Ashley, thought Markham sadly, was above and beyond it all.

Fear no more the heat o' the sun, nor the furious winter's rages.

Managing to squeeze with Noakes into a dark oak pew near the back, Markham caught sight of Olivia on the other side of the aisle, next to Matthew Sullivan and Harry Mountfield. She looked very pale and was shivering. As he watched, Harry Mountfield wrapped a burly arm gently round her, clamping the slender form to his side. At this, Markham almost seemed to hear a hiss as the green snake of jealousy detached itself from a side-window depicting the Garden of Eden and writhed towards him on undulating coils. It felt like a blasphemy against nature that he should not be the one to support his lover. Swallowing hard, he fought down the angry resentment and endeavoured to be glad that she had good friends by her side.

At that moment, Olivia caught sight of him and bowed gravely. The gesture seemed cruelly cold and unlike herself, piercing him like a steely point of agony, since its formality seemed to say that he was not yet forgiven. Matthew

Sullivan saw him too and raised a hand in salute. His eyes were sympathetic. Had Olivia told Matthew about the row, he wondered. Did her oldest friend feel she had been abominably wronged? Or did he have some fellow-feeling for Markham in the stormy fluctuation of his feelings?

Get a grip, he told himself fiercely. Desperately, he grasped the keys and other objects in his trouser pockets so hard that he thought he must draw blood.

There was a minor commotion at the back of the church.

The coffin had arrived.

As the congregation rose to its feet and the pall bearers carried their precious burden down the aisle, Markham tried not to think about the mutilated remains within. Instead, he scanned the mourners.

Strange how the trappings of woe had somehow diluted their individuality, so that even Helen Kavanagh seemed no more than a collection of black draperies topped by mottled purple-faced solemnity. Indeed, although he was a Roman Catholic, the whole ritual seemed somehow dream-like, the sensation that he was a spectator at something alien and ill-understood mysteriously mirroring his deep sense of loneliness.

A bird-like woman nearest the coffin whose tiny frame shook with grief was presumably the deceased's mother. A phalanx of heavy-featured relatives filled the front few rows. The remaining mourners appeared to be colleagues from Hope, with a sprinkling of startlingly good-looking young men also in attendance, their funeral weeds of a cut and dash which suggested designer labels.

The rows immediately in front of Markham's were filled with heavily made-up young girls clutching wilting bouquets, pictures of the deceased and, bizarrely, mobile phones. God, he thought wildly, surely they're not planning to start texting or taking selfies!

As the Requiem Mass proceeded, his worst fears went unrealized, the young women contenting themselves with a lachrymose chorus of sobs and snuffles by way of antiphonal contrast to the mumbling adjurations of the red-nosed elderly celebrant. There was a dangerous moment during the Eulogy, when a subdued ululating seemed to break out amongst them, but this gradually subsided like breakers retreating from the shingle.

The hazy feeling of unreality grew stronger. Perhaps he was coming down with something. Or maybe it was just a sense of moving in a dim and clogging medium. The air thick with incense and the scent of the lilies ...

Just as he felt he must pass out for want of air, there was a general stir and a wheezy organ struck up the recessional hymn.

Thank God.

And then Markham felt it. A prickling between his shoulder blades.

Suddenly, he was quite certain the killer was there in the church. Indistinguishable from his fellow mourners as to the external decencies, bowing his head respectfully to the coffin. Inwardly, his soul capering gleefully at the sight of Ashley Dean's pitiful remains moving inexorably towards their last home underground.

Markham's gaze swept the congregation as it shuffled out of the church. Beside him, he knew Noakes was doing the same. Looking for anything that jarred, that didn't fit.

But they wouldn't find it.

He was too clever for that.

High above, on a corbel in the transept, a gargoyle with a wicked little face looked down on the emptying church as if it possessed a secret that it would not share with them if it could.

The wake was held at an undistinguished little pub called The Halfway House which formed part of a terrace of shops just around the corner from the church.

Still the rain came down drearily, interminably.

As they followed the throng of mourners out of the church car park, Noakes waved his Order of Service at Markham.

'This says the burial's for close family only, Guv.' Jerking a thumb at the gaggle of young girls making frantic repairs to their mascara-streaked faces, he enquired, 'D'you think that lot are planning to gate-crash it or do owt daft?'

The DI scrutinized Ashley Dean's erstwhile groupies.

'I don't think we need fear a mass outbreak of suttee, Sergeant,' he remarked sardonically. Then, observing Noakes's bafflement, he added more compassionately, 'They're over the worst, poor things. With so many teachers around, they'll probably just slope off somewhere and do their own thing.'

This prediction appeared to be accurate. As they watched, the youthful female contingent of the mourning party peeled off towards the town centre, self-consciously clutching each other as they teetered along in their too-tight skirts and skyscraper stilettos, hair dripping in rats' tails over their shoulders.

The Halfway House was a typical chain hostelry, somewhat

dark and dismal as though the place was crying out for refurbishment. Vases of cheap plastic flowers were dotted around the private lounge area at strategic intervals – no doubt all part of the 'compassionate catering experience' discreetly advertised in the brochures that Markham had noticed stacked at reception. Bowls of peanut M&Ms stood on tables next to pictures of the deceased.

'His favourite treat,' whispered a glassy-eyed Tracey Roach gliding past Markham and making him jump.

At the back of the room, a buffet was set out with the standard finger food – sandwiches, vol au vents, slices of quiche, bowls of salad and other dainties, along with trays bearing glasses of red and white wine. A smaller table held tea, coffee and soft drinks. Markham's thoughts travelled back to the ravaged little woman who had stood weeping next to the coffin. It struck him as unbearably poignant that in the midst of her heartbreak she should have had to think about mundanities like menus and costs per head.

No such thoughts troubled Noakes whose eyes brightened as he surveyed the spread.

While others hung back, doubtless not wishing to appear precipitate in falling upon the eatables, the DS had no such compunction.

'We missed elevenses, Guv,' he murmured plaintively to Markham, clearly concerned lest the DI should be slow out of the starting blocks.

'Honestly man, do you ever think about *anything* except your stomach?'

Noakes was unruffled. 'Important to have fuel in the tank,' he riposted.

'Hmm, it's just that *you* seem to refuel several times a day.'

The DS's eyebrows made their pathetic angle.

'Oh, go on then, but for God's sake show some decorum. It's not an all-you-can-eat contest, remember.'

Needing no second urging, Noakes surged forward, shortly followed by others who felt that they could feast with propriety now that someone else had gone first.

'Not hungry, Gil?'

Matthew Sullivan's wry tones jolted Markham out of his reverie.

'Not really, Matt. As you see, Noakes is eating for two.'

'Him and the other Christian carnivora!'

Markham laughed then stiffened as he saw Olivia waylay Noakes who, blushing like a schoolboy, was obviously the butt of her gentle raillery. The DS looked guiltily over his shoulder, gesturing towards Markham with a cocktail sausage.

Olivia's eyes met those of her lover in a long level stare. As in the church, she gave a cool self-possessed nod and then turned aside, patting Noakes lightly on the arm as she melted away.

It was in keeping with Sullivan's innate sensitivity that he affected not to notice this little bit of byplay. Markham burned to know if Olivia had confided in her friend but was too proud to ask. Cut to the quick by her studied negation, he strove desperately to check any manifestation of pain. Noakes's arrival, balancing a pyramid of food, saved him. Expressively rolling his eyes to heaven, Sullivan left the two policemen to it.

'Sure you've got enough there, Sergeant?'

The sarcasm was water off a duck's back.

'I know what I like, an' I like what I know,' Noakes said happily, wolfing down vol au vents, crisps, coleslaw, and quiche indiscriminately.

Eventually, however, he paused for breath.

'Everything all right with, er, your … Olivia?' he blurted out awkwardly, keeping a wary eye on the guv'nor lest he be shot down in flames.

Markham was touched but fell back on his unconquerable reserve.

'We're working, Noakes, she understands that,' he said shortly.

'Right enough.' The DS devoured his wounded feeling along with the remainder of the quiche.

Suddenly, Markham wanted nothing so much as to escape the heaving throng.

'I'll be out there,' he said, moving towards the hallway.

Away from the lounge, it was mercifully cool and quiet. Looking through the window of the lighted lobby, the objects he turned his back on were still before him instead of the grass and trees.

Suddenly, in the reflected image he saw a motionless figure standing at the door of the lounge watching him. He couldn't see the face.

In that instant, he knew the watcher in the shadows was Ashley Dean's killer.

Markham whirled round, but there was no-one there.

In three strides, he was standing at the doorway of the lounge, raking it with his gaze.

'Are you all right, sir?' A fresh-faced girl with startling violet hair was looking up at him in concern.

The DI gathered his scattered wits. 'Fine, just looking for a friend,' he answered dismissively, relieved to see that Noakes was coming towards him.

'Nothing doing in there,' the DS grunted.

'Let's just pay our respects to Ashley's mother and go.'

'She won't be along any time soon, Guv. Collapsed at the cemetery, apparently. Her sister's taken her home.'

'That poor woman.' Markham's voice throbbed with pity.

Another suffering figure to swell the host who thronged his dreams, begging him to bring them closure and lay the evil to rest.

'Where to, Guv?' asked Noakes, suppressing a belch as he sat with Markham in the car park at Our Lady of the Angels.

'Back to the station, Sergeant. Let's take some time to regroup. Burton and Doyle can hold the fort for a while longer at Hope.'

As they slid into the rush-hour traffic, Markham's mind replayed the afternoon's proceedings. He had an uneasy feeling that he had missed something. It hovered on the periphery of his vision, but try as he might he could not grasp it.

Noakes seemed to read his mind.

'It's all that black, Guv,' he pronounced elliptically.

'How so, Sergeant?'

'Everyone looks the same, don't they? I mean, like them nuns from that convent place round the back of Bromgrove Uni.'

Markham was quite intrigued to see where this was leading.

'The Sisters of Saint Cecilia, Noakes? What about them?'

'Well, they all look like crows. My Muriel says she can't tell one from another cos the black getup makes them seem identical.'

Even allowing for Noakes's rooted anti-Papist prejudice, Markham had to admit that he had a point.

'Yes,' he mused, 'no-one stood out today... All the faces were blurred ... as if someone had gone over them with a smudge-stick.'

Noakes was gratified with the DI's reception of his hypothesis. That's one in the eye for smarty-pants Kate Burton, he thought.

Back at the station, they had barely hung their steaming jackets to dry on CID's temperamental radiator when the desk sergeant put his head round the door.

'DCI Sidney's wanting you, sir.' He grinned. 'Put out an All Ports Alert.'

Markham groaned.

'Oh God, that's all I need.' Hopefully he asked, 'Any chance of stalling him?'

'More than my life's worth, Inspector, if you know what I mean.'

Markham did know, all too well.

'OK, Noakes, better get up there.'

Slimy Sid's PA was usually an accurate barometer of the great man's mood. Today, the auguries were not good, Miss Peabody's hands alternately fingering her pearls and fluttering about her marcel-waved hair as though to propitiate an angry deity.

She did not meet Markham's eyes.

Another bad sign.

'Please go straight in, Inspector,' she said faintly.

Markham was aware of Noakes straightening his tie and sucking in his paunch.

Don't rise to Slimy Sid, he told himself. Whatever the bastard says, don't rise to it.

As it happened, DCI Sidney was not alone.

A stocky, bushy-haired man with the florid face of a drinker and curranty eyes was overflowing one of the four chairs at the conference table.

The DCI looked distinctly plethoric himself, reflected Markham, as he and Noakes seated themselves. Though in his case, it was likely to be the result of temper rather than anything of a bacchanalian nature. Even Sidney's bald dome seemed to shake out sparks of irritation, while a testy tugging at the salt and pepper beard boded ill for his subordinates.

'This is Mr Jed Harris, Parent Governor at Hope Academy, Inspector.' Sidney's tone was minatory. 'He wants to know what you are doing to find this ... this maniac. And so do I.'

'With respect, sir, it's been less than a week since Ashley Dean's murder—'

'And in that time another member of staff has been killed on your watch.' Sidney's voice dripped venom.

'Audrey Burke's death is being investigated with all possible expedition, sir.' Markham's reply was inflectionless.

Jed Harris's face was a picture of honest bewilderment.

'I'll not beat about the bush, Mr Markham. I want to know what the 'eck's going on at the school. Nobody'll give us the time of day 'cept the journos outside.'

Markham cursed Hope's senior leadership team. They were supposed to be liaising with the police press office but had clearly decided to pull up the drawbridge and ring down the portcullis. What a self-serving shower. Too busy with their damage-limitation exercise to reassure worried parents.

'I'm sorry parents haven't been properly briefed, Mr Harris. I don't believe there's any risk to students, particularly as it's half term next week.'

The big man heaved himself up and proffered a meaty paw.

'Appreciate it, Inspector. Just wanted to set the missus' mind at rest. What with staff going down like ninepins. You start imagining all sorts.'

As if in response to an invisible summons, Miss Peabody appeared.

The DCI was all unctuous solicitude. 'Be assured, Mr Harris, I am taking personal command of this investigation.'

Which means taking the credit if we get a result and selling us down the river if we don't, Markham's eyes telegraphed Noakes.

As soon as the door had shut behind the visitor, Sidney went on the attack, his voice rising several octaves and his complexion turning a deeper shade of puce.

'Now you listen to me, Markham. I want *results*, d'you hear me? *Results.*'

A vicious yank of the beard.

'This could have serious ramifications for community relations.'

Upset too many apple carts, in other words.

'Start looking at local mental hospitals. Mark my words, that's where you should be focusing your attention.' Sidney's eyes narrowed. 'And no harassment of James Palmer.'

'Of course not, sir.'

The DI's expression was guileless.

Noakes knew that look of old. It meant Markham intended to plough his own furrow and to hell with Slimy Sid.

The show of subservience appeared to satisfy the DCI who dismissed them with a flick of his wrist.

Miss Peabody hovered at the door, eyes downcast like the handmaid to a potentate.

'I'll want daily updates from now on.' Sidney's peevish tones followed them to the door and then, mercifully, faded away.

The two men stood in the corridor and contemplated each other glumly.

'I'll get on to Burton, Guv. Tell her to put a rocket under Kavanagh and the press office.'

Markham nodded gratefully, hardly trusting himself to speak, and the DS padded away on his errand.

Wheels within wheels, thought Markham. He would have to give the appearance of keeping the DCI in the loop while secretly going his own way.

Hope Academy would remain the focus of his search, not some sodding mental health facility.

Back in CID, it felt as though the temperature had dropped. The DI shivered. He felt somehow at the mercy of centrifugal forces whirling him further and further away from the truth. Then he braced himself. Let battle commence!

With the effect of a sharp concussion, he remembered there would be no Olivia waiting at home to take the sting out of Slimy Sid's bromides. How he ached for her comforting presence now.

Outside the wind keened sorrowfully. Markham could only hope it was not sounding another death knell.

10

The Eye of the Storm

THE HASTILY CONVENED PRESS conference hadn't gone too badly, thought Markham late that evening as he massaged his aching temples, eyes screwed up against the harsh glare of the electric light.

He'd given a masterclass in equivocation that Slimy Sid himself could hardly have bettered – wall to wall platitudes and the usual guff about pursuing several lines of inquiry. Noakes had sat next to him, his lugubrious gravedigger's expression striking the requisite note of solemnity.

The DI could tell that sharp-elbowed wide boy from the *Bromgrove Gazette* hadn't really bought it, but he stuck manfully to the script, the reference to 'a seriously disturbed individual' sufficiently vague as to include both local nutters and suspects closer to home.

Thankfully, none of the hacks appeared to have got a whiff of Olivia's involvement, and he intended to keep it that way. Without actually lying, he hadn't corrected the assumption that a cleaner had discovered Ashley Dean's body. The DCI was liable to go off at the deep end if Markham's personal life became the story, but tonight's fudge should keep the vultures at bay. For a while, anyway. Noakes and Doyle had been tasked with escorting the visitors 'safely off the premises.' He could trust them to ensure that no-one took the scenic route!

Before the press conference, there had been another staff briefing. Just as at Ashley's funeral, James Palmer was conspicuous by his absence. Markham caught the tail end of some muttered conversations – 'ashamed to show his face ... no smoke without fire ... what's he got to hide?' – which suggested that ill-feeling was mounting against the head. Or was it being cleverly stoked, he wondered. And, if so, by whom? A subdued Tracey Roach barely raised her eyes, while the rest looked equally shell-shocked. There was a brief ripple when Helen Kavanagh announced that she would be taking over as acting head *pro tem*, but this quickly died away. Markham's recital of the bare facts about Audrey Burke's murder was received in tense silence before a low murmuring broke out. Dave Uttley stood at some distance from his colleagues, grey-faced and lost in thought. Doctor Abernathy plucked distractedly at the sleeves of his academic gown, while a sallow young man whose lanyard proclaimed him to be the deputy facilities manager bounced nervously on the balls of his feet as he hovered behind the new acting head awaiting instructions.

Afterwards, as the gathering dispersed, Matthew Sullivan ambled across to speak to the DI. Markham registered that the teacher was looking uncharacteristically drawn, his features almost emaciated. He reckoned Doctor Abernathy had noticed it too from the look of concern he directed at his young colleague on leaving the briefing.

'Never made much of an effort with Audrey,' he said with quiet sincerity. 'And now it's too late.'

Markham had inwardly been wrapping his soul in cold reserve, prepared to rebuff any approach to the subject of his girlfriend. It was a relief to his shrinking sensitivity that Sullivan clearly didn't intend to speak about the rupture with Olivia.

The reprieve was almost too great for him to feel anything else, but Markham nevertheless strove to find some words of comfort.

'I'm sure a great many people here would say the same.'

'Still, it's no excuse. We all took her for granted.' A muscle jumped at the corner of Sullivan's mouth. 'And now look at us. More concerned with ourselves than Audrey.'

Timor mortis conturbat me.

Harry Mountfield had been watching them and now threaded his way through the crush of bodies. As Kavanagh swept by on a wave of Hugo Boss *pour femme*, he grimaced. 'You won't get far quoting "No man is an island" to that one, Matt!'

Sullivan gave a short laugh. 'Too right.' He turned to Markham. 'Audrey had a life, maybe not a great one, but it was taken away from her. See you get whoever did it,' he said before allowing Mountfield to draw him away.

Helen Kavanagh's high-wattage insincerity was at full throttle.

'I simply *must* check how JP is coping. He shouldn't *think* of getting back in the saddle when he must be *in pieces* about Ashley,' she trilled.

'And Audrey,' added Markham drily, gratified to note that Kavanagh had the grace to look somewhat discomfited.

He was willing to bet she had somehow brought pressure to bear on the LEA, resulting in Slimy Sid's recent fatwa. *Hands off Hope*, had been the message. Well, we'll see about that.

Two more days to half term. Then at least the premises would be free of kids milling around.

He frowned. The autopsy reports on both Ashley and Audrey had made it clear they couldn't rule anyone out.

Even a woman. Or a teenager.

Who were those lads who had been excluded after an altercation with Ashley Dean? The ones who'd accused him of being JP's bumboy?

Their alibis needed checking.

Plus, they needed to encourage any victims of bullying by Ashley Dean to come forward.

Perhaps Matthew Sullivan or, better still, Harry Mountfield could help there as they seemed to have the kids' trust.

'I don't want to come over all *Dead Poets* on you,' Mountfield had told them, 'but the truth is I just want to give some of these poor little sods a better song to sing.'

Despite his ingrained cynicism, Markham had been touched. Mountfield clearly had faith in all the Laurens, Nickis and Jakes, seeing beyond the bluster and bravado to the frightened waifs beneath. Watching him with the young-sters at break time – joshing dull-eyed lads and coaxing a smile from even the tartiest teenage jezebels – Markham had the feeling that this was a man who really *cared*.

So many tasks to be actioned.

Sisyphus.

Markham felt heavy-headed and sluggish, as though all the oxygen had been sucked out of his body. How did staff stand being stuck in the bunker all day? His thoughts turned to Olivia – a caged songbird in this airless aviary …

There was a knock.

DC Burton's shiny, burnished head appeared round the door.

Markham dredged up a welcoming smile.

'Come in, Kate.'

Burton perched on a chair. That was one of her traits, he'd observed – she never made herself properly comfortable, but always sat bolt upright and alert as though it would somehow be a dereliction of duty to let her spine touch the back of a seat.

'Where're we up to with pupil statements? The boys who'd … had issues with Ashley Dean?'

The notebook was flipped open before he had finished speaking.

'Declan Thompson, Callum Smith and George Hickson,' she rattled off. 'Alibied by their mums for both murders, sir.'

'Hmm, weak alibis then. What's the betting the three musketeers had their stories off pat well before we came calling?'

Burton smiled weakly. 'More than likely. They all live in Hugh Gaitskell House on the Hoxton.'

The Hoxton. Bromgrove's notorious sink estate. Popularly known as Scrote Central.

'What was your impression, Kate, having seen them in their "natural habitat"?'

The DC's expression was queasy.

'Pretty much your typical teenage lowlifes, sir. Lots of homophobic digs at Ashley, the head, Mr Sullivan and a few others.'

Sullivan. Now that *was* interesting.

'They didn't have a good word for anyone at Hope except for Harry Mountfield. Had the odd kickabout with him, apparently.' Unexpectedly, she grinned. 'They seemed to have a soft spot for Doctor Abernathy too. Said he was,' she consulted her jottings, 'mad as a box of frogs, but a nice old git.'

'Perhaps here's hope for them yet, then,' said Markham.

'I wouldn't hold your breath, sir. From what the neighbours said, they're real tearaways.'

'But not killers?'

Burton chewed her lip and fiddled with her pen.

'I don't think so, sir,' she said cautiously. 'The boys were upfront about loathing Ashley – said whoever offed him deserved a medal – but they seemed as shocked as everyone else. And there wasn't a flicker when I mentioned Audrey. Declan even asked if she was the bird with the big boobs who came round when they wagged school. I think he meant the Attendance Officer ... it was obvious none of them had a clue who Audrey was.'

Markham digested this information.

'What about the student who was supposedly being bullied by Ashley?' he asked wearily.

'Pete Clarke.' Burton shook her head. 'He looks like a stiff breeze'd blow him over, Guv.'

She checked her notes. 'He admitted Ashley was throwing his weight around – making snide remarks about him being a nancy boy stoner – but he seemed quite cool about it, so I reckon Declan and the other two were just using it as an excuse to have a go at Ashley.'

'Anything useful from other students?'

'Nothing, sir.' Again, she shook her head sorrowfully, the soulful brown eyes heightening her resemblance to a miniature dachshund. Markham half expected her to sit up and beg.

'All alibied, I suppose?'

'To the hilt, and nothing flagged up on the statements as far as we can see.'

'So, Ashley had a sadistic streak – took a delight in tormenting people. But, from the sound of it, we're not looking for someone from the student population?'

'S'pose it's possible.' Burton sounded dubious. 'Or maybe an adult manipulated one of the kids into acting as an accomplice ...'

The DI's brooding gaze was despondent.

What are we missing, he asked himself for the umpteenth time. Was some maniac on the loose, corrupting teenagers like a psychopathic Pied Piper? Did the key to the murders lie somewhere in Ashley's past? What had he done to merit such a hideous end? Where did Audrey fit in? The questions pounded his brain like insistent hammers on an anvil.

A soft cough alerted him to Burton, waiting deferentially for further insights.

Clearly she saw him as some sort of reincarnation of Inspector Morse, he thought irritably, when he felt a million miles removed from such sphinx-like omniscience.

The DC coughed again as if she had something difficult to say. A rush of colour streamed into her cheeks.

'D'you fancy a drink, sir? To take your mind off the case.'

The question hung in the air between them, the silence suddenly charged with meaning.

Burton's big brown eyes were full of abject supplication.

Damn, damn and double damn! Markham cursed himself for a blind fool. He should have seen this coming. Now he had to let her down tactfully, kindly, without damaging the professional trust between them.

'I'll have to pass tonight, I'm afraid, Kate.' He strove for an avuncular tone, ignoring the unspoken message her eyes were sending him. 'I'm too bushed to be great company. Besides, my girlfriend will be waiting for me.' Perhaps by saying this, he could make it a reality. 'You, Noakes and Doyle can raise a glass to me.'

The DC's cheeks were a painful scarlet.

'S'all right, sir.' Her voice was small. 'You must want to get off.'

At that moment, the door banged open and Noakes slouched into the room.

'That Gavin Conors from the *Gazette*!' he raged. 'Took me an' Doyle half an hour to get shut of him. Kept doubling back an' giving us the slip, cocky little git.' He scowled darkly. 'Jim Snell's a waste of space an' all. Just left us to it, the idle dipshit—'

Markham interrupted the angry monologue.

'I'm off now, Sergeant. All done in.' He looked hard at Noakes. '*Olivia will be waiting for me.*' He flourished a twenty at the DS. 'I want the team to have a drink on me. You've worked hard today.'

Noakes's gaze ping ponged from Markham to the crimson-faced Burton.

He sized up the situation in an instant.

'Right-o, Guv,' he replied, bestowing on the hapless DC a look in which malicious enjoyment and native guile were strongly blended. 'C'mon, luv, get your coat. We're wasting valuable drinking time!'

Markham dragged his way leadenly up the flight of shallow stone steps at the front of The Sweepstakes, then on through the marble-tiled lobby and across to the lift which would whisk him up to his apartment.

It felt like an age since he had last set foot in it.

Opening the front door to number 56, his heart gave a great lurch when he saw light spilling out from the living room.

Olivia.

As he entered the room, he saw her rise swiftly from the armchair where she had been sitting. How pale and wretched she looked! Her hands were clasping and unclasping in some kind of nervous apprehension. What would she do? As though in answer to his unspoken question, she came to him, and drew him over to her vacated chair. Then she moved a foot-stool next to him, and sat there in silence for a moment. When eventually she spoke, it was with quiet fervour.

'Gil, I'm sorry for the way I spoke to you, and for storming out as I did. But you don't know ... When you mentioned that boy, and what I was supposed to have done, I thought I'd lost you.'

Markham's heart was too full for speech.

Olivia seemed to read the history of her lover's sleepless night and agonized self-questioning in his shattered looks.

Her voice, tremulous till then, gained some of its old confident firmness as she continued, her hand resting upon his knee.

'There *was* a sixth-former, Gil, a boy who had a crush on me. I was giving him extra help but stopped the lessons the minute I realized.' She sighed. 'Apparently, he "told all" to his parents, even though there was nothing to tell. Anyway, they didn't take it very well and turned it all round to make it look as though *I* had come on to *him.'*

'Darling, there's no need—'

Olivia seemed not to hear him.

'Luckily,' she continued, 'I'd kept JP informed from the start, so he and the governors had to back me.' Her hand tightened on Markham's knee. 'It was embarrassing, because two of the governors were friends of the parents, and there was some spiteful gossip. Schools can be real snake pits sometimes ...'

Hearing how she gained in confidence as she told him of her ordeal, Markham felt as if some icy pressure had melted and his consciousness had room to expand. Olivia had come back to him.

'I don't know how to begin to apologize, Liv,' he faltered. 'This case ...'

It hath cowed my better part of man.

Olivia stroked his exhausted face.

'It's all right, Gil. I don't blame you for wondering ... You see, I know what Cheryl's like.' Her voice was scornful. 'What else did she say?' It was safe, she knew, to ask that question now.

'Just that you'd seen the lad socially after he left Hope,' replied Markham, the blood coming and going painfully in his dark face.

'*Socially*? *Hardly*! I met him for the last time at the Leavers' Prom along with half a dozen or so other teachers. I was never alone with him – took bloody good care not to be!' Olivia's tone was vehement, and Markham realized that his girlfriend was starting to resent her apparent need to justify herself. However, she suddenly fell quiet, and Markham determined that he would not speak until she had driven out of her soul the lingering traces of resentment.

It had begun to rain heavily again, great gusts dashing against the window as though some angry demon was launching an attack on their apartment. Inside, however, all was peace.

It was a while before Olivia spoke again, her voice very low so that Markham had to stoop to hear her.

'Ashley Dean enjoyed taunting me about the whole affair, Gil. That's how he got his kicks. Breaking people like butterflies on a wheel.' Markham winced. It was a vivid analogy.

He gently caressed the heavy coil of hair which seemed almost too heavy for the fragile neck, revelling in the sense of confidence and happy freedom which he thought to have lost forever.

'I'm so sorry about Audrey,' Olivia continued with mounting agitation, rising abruptly from the footstool. 'When Matt rang me with the news, I couldn't take it in. The poor woman didn't have much of a life outside school. Looked after her mother who had dementia ... Oh God, what'll happen to her mum now?'

Markham wouldn't, *couldn't* describe what he and Burton had found, but Olivia must have caught the reflection of it in his haunted expression. She put a finger to his lips. 'I can wait until you're ready.'

Her lover wondered if he would *ever* be ready.

'Whoever it was, we'll find them,' he said simply. 'Audrey almost certainly got hold of some clue to the killer's identity. Instead of coming to us, she took a terrible gamble ... and lost.'

Olivia came to a decision.

'Right, enough of Hope Academy for one night. Let's get out for a bit. We could try The Grapes. Should be fairly quiet mid-week.'

Markham felt a regenerating shudder pass through his frame. Smiling back at her, he said, 'Sounds like a plan.'

The Grapes was an unpretentious old-fashioned pub with a few plain deal tables in the front room next to the bar. Behind this was a smaller, more intimate room lined with oak booths, allowing patrons to escape the madding crowd.

Markham and Olivia paused briefly in the main lounge, its sober antique brasses and warming pans in startling contrast to a carpet patterned in swirling red and black fleur-de-lis. 'Makes a real style statement,' the landlady Denise had sighed happily to Markham who privately thought the clashing décor more likely to trigger a migraine.

The place was quiet for a weekday, with only a few drinkers at the bar. In the stone inglenook to the right of the counter an open fire crackled cheerfully, its flames reflected in a vast array of tankards and flagons suspended on hooks above the gnarled old mantelpiece. A mournful-looking bulldog surveyed the clientele from his position in front of the fire, its muzzle twitching hopefully at savoury odours suggestive of chops.

With its twisted beams, blocked up chimney pieces and funny little partitions of which no-one seemed to know the purpose, The Grapes was decidedly not one of Bromgrove's chicest eateries, but Markham and Olivia loved the place for its arthritic charm and imperviousness to gentrification.

The back room with banquette seating being much more to their taste, by mutual consent they headed to their favourite table at the far end. All was as dark and warm as they could wish for, a smaller log fire casting leaping shadows over the creaking, sloping-floored interior.

After some deliberation over the menu, Markham went off to the bar to place their order and collect drinks.

'Like Captain Oates, I may be gone some time,' he told Olivia.

The landlady's partiality for Markham was a running joke between them. Convinced that no-one could be half good enough for her 'favourite policeman', it had been a while before Denise unbent to Markham's girlfriend, but Olivia now seemed to have passed some sort of undefined probation as signified by sundry approving nods and winks.

She snuggled back into the booth, stretching luxuriously. The reconciliation with Markham left her feeling almost light-headed with joy, as though she had narrowly escaped some torture screw.

Suddenly, Olivia heard a familiar voice and stiffened.

It was Jessica Clark, one of the secretaries from Hope,

normally a colourless mouse of a woman but clearly buoyed up on this occasion by a cocktail or three.

Snatches of speech floated across to her.

'... Matthew Sullivan ... yes, that's the one ... teaches English and Drama ...'

Another female voice said something indistinguishable. Jessica shrieked with affected laughter which set Olivia's teeth on edge.

'You'd be wasting your time, Jules. He's gay.'

Again, some muffled response followed by another banshee cackle.

'... If truth be told, our Mr Sullivan had the hots for poor Ashley Dean.'

Having scooped up the requisite tribute of oohs and ahhs – as though spooning up jelly, thought Olivia viciously – Jessica became salaciously conspiratorial.

'Well, Ashley wasn't going to waste himself on a *teacher*. The head was nuts about him, see, so poor Matt got the boot. Marcia in Accounts said him and Ashley had a *fearful* quarrel. The door was open so she couldn't help hearing. Matt said something about Ashley being – excuse my French –,' coy titter, 'a sick fuck who'd made him think they had something special.'

Olivia winced with pain, belatedly realizing she was pressing the tines of a fork into her palm.

'Oh yeah, Ash swung both ways ... a real flirt ... wouldn't have kicked him out of bed ... must've been terrible for Matt seeing him every day ... Marce said if looks could kill ...'

A clatter of coffee cups intervened, drowning the babble.

Olivia peeped around the corner of the booth.

Thank God. Jessica and her companion, a blowsy looking woman she vaguely recalled having seen in the Council's Education offices, were shrilly divvying up their bill.

Go, just go!

As though in answer to her prayers, Jessica's strident tones died away.

Olivia shut her eyes and sank back against the red velvet seating.

She knew Matt was gay, but had never suspected him of being involved with Ashley.

It must have happened when she moved from Hope to take the job at St Mary's. Neither Matt nor Harry had ever breathed a word of it to her. For a moment, she felt hurt but then reproached herself for a fool. Matt had a proud sensitivity which would have made Ashley Dean's rejection bitter as gall. Highly unlikely he would have broached the painful topic even with Harry ...

'Gil to Olivia! Come back to me, sweetheart!'

Olivia became aware that Markham was looking down at her, his expression quizzical.

'You were far away, Liv.' Then, noticing her pallor, 'What is it? What's wrong?'

He slid into the seat opposite and set down their drinks before reaching for her hand.

Haltingly, Olivia recounted what she had overheard, the words choking on her tongue.

Markham listened attentively.

'Oh Gil,' she said, vainly trying to subdue the pulse of apprehension beating inside her, 'this changes everything, doesn't it?'

'It's a complication, certainly,' he replied evenly. 'But then, Liv, nothing about this case is straightforward.'

The trustful look in her eyes went straight to his heart.

'Listen, dearest, tonight we are going to forget that damned school. Forget what that harpy said. It's all hearsay. Keep faith with your friend.'

Markham spoke with a confidence that he did not feel.

Things looked black for Sullivan, he reflected.

Sex was somehow at the heart of this. But whose lust had curdled and turned murderous? JP's? Sullivan's? Or was there someone else – a chameleon able to fade into the background at will?

The thought sent a rush of acrid bile into his stomach.

Let me get to him before he claims another victim.

11

Secrets

As he crossed Hope's forecourt with Noakes on Thursday morning, Markham was confronted by a gaggle of reporters lying in wait.

'Once we're inside, get Doyle to deal with them,' he instructed Noakes crisply. 'Usual pack drill – ongoing investigations, no comment, another press conference at the appropriate time, yada yada.'

'Must be a slow news day, Guv.' The DS scowled at a couple of hacks from the *Gazette* before barreling through the pack like a bellicose silverback.

'Oi, mate,' shouted one journo in outrage, 'that's my foot you just trod on!'

A sly smirk overspread Noakes's features. Clearly, his size twelves had scored a bullseye.

Neither man said anything until they had reached the sanctuary of their temporary HQ where Burton and Doyle were already waiting. Noakes dispatched Doyle on his errand before brewing up, all the while observing Markham out of the corner of his eye. The guv'nor and Olivia must've kissed and made up, he concluded, noticing that some of the strain had left the boss's face. A peek at Burton's downcast expression confirmed that she had clocked it too. Good. No more come-on glances. The daft bint had finally got the message. Markham and Olivia were made for each other. Yin and yang, soul mates, like it said in those horoscope thingies he sometimes sneaked a look at ...

'Mission accomplished, Guv.' Doyle had made short work of his assignment. 'The press lot have cleared off. I've told reception to close the gates to the car park until going home time. If anyone needs access, there's the intercom.'

'Excellent.' It was the old decisive Markham. 'Right, here are the priorities for today. We'll get Palmer back in. And Matthew Sullivan needs to be re-interviewed.'

Succinctly, without mentioning Olivia, the DI disclosed what had emerged regarding Sullivan.

'So, *Sullivan* could've been the third man then, sir.' Burton's voice hummed with suppressed excitement. 'What if *he* wrote that letter we found in Ashley's locker – the slushy one that looked like it came from the head? He could've planted it to frame JP.' Two spots of colour appeared on her cheeks. 'What if *he* was the one who wanted Ashley dead? What if—'

'Let's not get ahead of ourselves here, Detective,' Markham gently reproved her, though with an inward smile at her enthusiasm. 'It could just as easily be someone else trying to frame Palmer ... or Sullivan for that matter. Either of them could have enemies we don't know about.'

'But now we know Sullivan's gay, he's our best bet surely,

sir?' Burton strove to keep her tone deferential, but was obviously champing at the bit.

Doyle looked up from his tea.

'What about the money angle? Maybe all the … er … sex stuff doesn't have owt to do with it.'

Burton was visibly irritated that the PC had thrown a spanner in the works. While privately agreeing with her that Sullivan looked good as a suspect, some demon of perversity made Noakes weigh in on Doyle's side of the debate.

''Appen you could be right, lad. Didn't you say the accounts looked a bit dodgy?'

Doyle looked owlish, squinting as he gathered his thoughts.

'I dunno, to be honest. From what I could see, it looked like there were perks and bungs going out. Corporate branding or some such. An' some of the teachers were having a whinge about it in the common room. Saying it was dead unfair how money was being wasted left, right and centre when they'd got nothing for books and printing.' Doyle paused then added, 'They sounded really angry, but clammed up when they saw me earwigging.'

'Hmm.' Markham looked at the young constable consideringly, causing him to flush unbecomingly to the roots of his ginger thatch. 'A pound to a penny, Hope's managers have been living high on the hog in approved CEO fashion. I wouldn't put it past them to have given us dummy accounts. Let's get Fraud to take a look, though I suspect Helen Kavanagh will have an answer for everything.'

'That poor sod Dave Uttley would have been putty in Kavanagh's hands,' opined Noakes. 'Prob'ly signed off on all sorts of stuff without having a clue.'

Burton was clearly reluctant to surrender her theory of a *crime passionnel*. 'I suppose it's possible,' she said grudgingly. 'Kavanagh certainly seems to think she's a cut above the little people.'

'Yeah, her office is something else. Looked like it cost shedloads of cash,' Noakes concurred.

The rich man in his castle, The poor man at his gate, God made them high and lowly, And ordered their estate.

'Mebbe they were all in on it,' growled Noakes, 'then Ashley got greedy and put the squeeze on the others.'

'Could be,' replied Markham. 'When thieves fall out, anything's possible.' He turned to Burton. 'Right, Kate, I want you to take Matthew Sullivan. Doyle can sit in and observe.'

He didn't dare risk Noakes trampling all over the man's sensibilities. Burton had sufficient tact and finesse to handle the interview. Besides, knowing her pride was in tatters after the other night, this was one way to signal his faith in her professionalism.

'Find out what was going on between Sullivan and Ashley. Don't go in all guns blazing, not at this stage. Just give the impression you're re-checking statements. Sullivan's alibied for the two murders—'

'Not water-tight, sir,' interrupted Burton. 'He was down the pub with his mates the evening of Ashley's murder. But they were all bladdered and no-one could be positive he was there the whole time.'

Markham frowned.

'What about when Audrey disappeared?'

'He was doing Intervention with various kids that afternoon.'

In answer to the DI's interrogative expression, she hastily expanded. 'That's when weaker students go to teachers for one-on-one help.'

'So, no-one to confirm if he was in his room the whole time.'

'That's right, sir. He could've slipped away for a bit and no-one would be any the wiser. The Intervention kids have special needs, so they're not exactly reliable. Usually there'd have been a teaching assistant around, but for some reason no-one seems to know who was covering the Intervention rota.' She rubbed her temples. 'They could have been under-staffed ...'

'Or Sullivan could have got rid of the TA on some pretext or other,' Markham quietly concluded. 'Easy enough to do if there was no fixed timetable and the kids just drifted in when they felt like it.'

The room fell silent. Outside, a solitary thrush chirruped as though to mock their gloomy thoughts.

Markham smiled bracingly at his team, though he felt far from confident. The case seemed increasingly like an impene-trable maze. He had to grasp every thread in the desperate hope that it would lead to the malignity buried at the heart of Hope Academy.

He turned to the DS. 'On your feet, Noakes. We're going to rouse Palmer from his sickbed. First stop, Helen Kavanagh's office. She can call Cheryl Palmer for us and find out how JP's doing.' He grimaced. 'No point doing anything on the QT. Kavanagh'll be on the blower to DCI Sidney screaming police oppression unless we square her beforehand.'

'How're you going to do that, Guv?' Noakes looked dubious.

'By downplaying any notion that JP or anyone else at Hope

is in the frame.' Markham's distaste was evident in the curl of his lip. 'By suggesting we're looking at the wider community – checking out anyone with an axe to grind, local bad boys, disturbed individuals, stalkers, that kind of thing. We imply that we're just tapping into JP's local knowledge.' He sighed in disgust. 'There's no chance of getting near him otherwise. If he thinks he's off the hook, there's a chance he'll relax and say something incriminating ... or blow the lid off whatever's going on here.'

'What if he gets lawyered up an' stays shtum?'

'Then we're stuffed.' Markham sounded resigned. 'But it's worth a shot. Come on, look sharpish. The bell for the end of period two will be going soon.'

In the event, these elaborate precautions were redundant.

As the two men approached Helen Kavanagh's office, Markham saw that the door was open.

JP's voice drifted out into the corridor, ragged with emotion.

Swiftly, the DI put out a detaining arm to hold Noakes back.

Standing stock still, they listened intently.

'It's a fucking nightmare, Helen, whichever way you look at it.'

'Well, obviously, you've been a bloody fool, but Wonder Boy's crew are chasing their tails. So long as you keep your mouth shut, they've got nothing.' Helen Kavanagh's voice was like a steel trap, all treacliness gone.

'I couldn't help it. I *loved* him. And then there was no way out.'

'He *played* you.' The words were freezing water droplets.

There was a groan like that of a wounded animal caught in a trap.

'You're a heartless bitch, you know.'

'I'm not going to let you bring me down with your mid-life faggot shenanigans. I've worked too hard for this.' The deputy head was implacable.

'He had us all by the short hairs, y'know. You, me and … well, I won't name names.' It was a thin whine.

'And he got his comeuppance, the poisonous little shit. When I heard the news, I wondered, is it too early to open a bottle?'

The raw hatred in her voice was shocking.

'It's too late to develop a conscience about this, JP. Get that tame quack of yours to buy us some time. I can't stall Markham forever. The man's no fool.' Kavanagh's voice took on an edge of bitter humour. 'Unlike his boss.'

Suddenly, the school bell shrilled.

Markham signaled peremptorily to Noakes.

Stealthily, they backed up, hardly daring to breathe until they had rounded the corner.

The corridor adjacent to Helen Kavanagh's office was heaving with students careering in a mad stampede to the canteen for their break-time bacon butties. Noakes sniffed the air hopefully, but one look at the DI's set expression told him there was no chance of making a detour to collect some emergency supplies.

Back in their own cubby-hole, the DI strode across to the window before whirling round upon Noakes.

'What the hell did we hear back there?' he enquired vehemently. 'A *confession*?'

'Sounded pretty much like it, Guv.' The DS thudded into a chair and regarded Markham meditatively, fitting his spatulate fingertips together with a degree of precision as though by this method he could somehow solve the conundrum. Then he shook his head thoughtfully, his shaggy brows going up and down like a doleful mastiff's. 'Though, come to think of it, Guv, JP didn't actually *admit* to killing Ashley ... only implied they'd, er, been in a relationship.'

Markham's intent expression showed that his mind was tumultuously busy.

'JP was involved in a homosexual affair, presumably with Ashley Dean. It also sounded like Ashley was holding something over him and Kavanagh—'

Noakes held up an admonitory finger. 'An' someone else too. Remember, JP said summat about not naming names.'

'Yes ... it could have been to do with money, if Ashley knew about people dipping into the kitty ... or sex, if he was threatening to expose gay colleagues.' Markham's manner was animated. Perhaps at last they were getting somewhere.

The DS too was alert with interest, his head cocked on one side as he pondered different scenarios.

'Mebbe JP had a fight with Ashley an' ended up killing him by accident – p'raps Ashley fell an' knocked his head ... Then someone else came by later – someone who hated Ashley's guts – and worked the body over, cut it up an' that ...' His voice tailed away as he saw the sceptical look on Markham's face. 'It's a long shot, I know, Guv,' he said humbly.

'No, you're right to think outside the box,' the DI said kindly. 'And it's quite true that JP didn't say anything which could tie him directly to the killing.'

Noakes brightened at the praise.

'What did JP mean by saying there was no way out, Guv?'

'That's the million dollar question, Noakesy. Whatever it was, Helen Kavanagh knew all about it. She'd hit the career jackpot, knowing all JP's sordid little secrets.'

'You mean …'

'Yes, I think Palmer got out of the clutches of one sadist only to end up at the mercy of another. Kavanagh doesn't care whether JP murdered Ashley or not. All she cares about is parlaying what she knows into a headship.'

The DS looked as if new vistas were opening before his eyes. Peering into the abyss, he voiced the appalling possibility.

'What if *Kavanagh* was the killer, Guv?'

'A woman could have done it. Kavanagh's certainly ruthless enough. But she's not the type to get her hands dirty … which isn't to say she couldn't have been involved …'

'Where does Sullivan fit into all this?' Noakes knuckled his forehead as though to subdue a host of suspects thronging his brain.

'I don't know, I just don't know.'

Markham was pensive. At first, he'd liked Matthew Sullivan for Olivia's sake. Later, as he had seen more of the lanky drama teacher, he had liked him for his own. Please God let him have nothing to do with this.

'There's Audrey's murder to consider as well,' he said sombrely. 'Maybe that's what JP meant when he said there was no way out.'

Things bad begun make strong themselves by ill.

At that moment, Burton and Doyle joined them.

162

'Matt Sullivan's out today doing a drama workshop with students at the Bromgrove Playhouse, sir,' Burton said. 'Do you want us to nip down there and bring him back?'

'No, Kate, we'll let Sullivan alone for the moment. We know where he is. You can do the interview as soon as he returns to school.'

Doyle appeared disappointed. No doubt hankering for some action with the blues and twos, Markham thought, with an inward smile. A thought occurred to him.

'What news of Jim Snell?'

Burton gave a snort of derision. 'Always doing a disappearing act. Along with his pals Jack Daniels and Johnnie Walker.'

'Hmm. Even so, I want to see him. Sozzled or not, he's the caretaker. They're the gatekeepers – nothing gets past them. Plus, Snell's a man with a grudge. I want to hear everything he can tell us about Ashley Dean.'

'Doyle and I had a peek in Snell's hidey-hole yesterday,' Noakes offered. 'The place was a total tip. You'd think the school caretaker would take a bit more pride. Glamour pics and porno mags all over the place.'

Doyle chipped in. 'Yeah, sir, it was really grungy. He must be keeping KFC and Bargain Booze in business single-handed, there were that many takeaway cartons and cans. And it had a dead peculiar smell. Like he'd been keeping an animal in there.'

'No self-respect, lad. Sign of the times.' Noakes sniffed virtuously. 'All those manky newspapers too. When there's a perfectly good recycling point round the back.'

'When you've quite finished comparing notes on the

caretaker's environmental credentials, I'd like him located, Sergeant.' Markham's voice was tart. 'Take Burton and Doyle with you. If Snell's sloped off somewhere, speak to Tracey Roach. With that sharp nose of hers, she'll soon winkle him out.'

Left alone, Markham's thoughts skittered uneasily, like scavengers' claws across a cellar floor.

Snell. The ferrety, rancid little man with beady eyes set too close together. How long had he been at Hope? Since forever, according to Olivia. As he sat there, her pungent pen-picture came back to him.

'Jim Snell really hates women, especially "uppity types". He had two wives who took him to the cleaners. Then there was some weird business with a mail-order Thai bride who vanished from the scene around six months ago. Ashley Dean flirted with her like crazy the one and only time Snell brought her to a staff shindig, which might have been one reason the course of true love never did run smooth. Sucks up to the senior leadership big time but doesn't give the rest of us the time of day. Functioning alcoholic and all round creep. Hoards snippets of gossip in that dingy little den like Hope's version of Gollum.'

Hoarder of gossip.

Keeper of secrets.

Snell was like a spider spinning webs from his lair deep within the school. But what if he had miscalculated? What if the spider encountered a predator the likes of which he could never have envisaged?

Markham's stomach lurched.

He had taken his eye off the ball with Audrey Burke. And

now here was Jim Snell gone to ground.

The DI fought to bring his hammering heart under control. Snell's duties would take him all over the school campus.

With mounting unease, he recalled Tracey Roach's words when they first arrived at the school. He had asked which areas were out of bounds to students. 'Hope's full of nooks and crannies,' she had told him airily. 'It's a real labyrinth in the basement. Jim Snell's the only one who knows his way around down there.'

Markham's thoughts were rudely interrupted as the door to the office rocked on its hinges.

'*Guv!*' There was an urgency about Noakes which made Markham's stomach swill and his mouth go dry. 'Guv, we need you to take a look at Snell's office.'

For once Noakes had not exaggerated. The smell was an appalling amalgam of dried-up food, mould, Strongbow, Rothmans, festering laundry, soiled kebab wrappers and other odours that Markham preferred not to identify. A small gas ring overflowed with a gelatinous tar-like slick on which a greasy saucepan balanced forlornly like some culinary Wreck of the Hesperus.

By dint of taking shallow breaths through his mouth, Markham managed to avoid gagging. Burton, standing next to the rickety desk where she and Doyle had been sifting through a tidal wave of newspapers and yellowing bits of papers, grimaced in sympathy.

'Snell must have been camping out in here, Guv. The poor sod seems to have hit rock bottom.'

Markham glanced round the frowsy cubicle. Bare-breasted nymphets simpered from the *Nuts 2011 Glamour Girls*

Official UK Wall Calendar as though to mock the incineration of Snell's romantic dreams, while a stack of top-shelf magazines spoke eloquently of his unholy lifestyle. The DI felt a stab of pity along with the revulsion. "'There but for the grace of God go all of us.'"

'What a slob!' Noakes quipped wanly. 'Makes *Benefits Street* look like Buckingham Palace.'

Burton gestured to what looked like a pile of ash.

'Looks like Snell was burning something in here, sir.'

Whipping a pair of tweezers out of her pocket, she gently extracted a thin strip of charred paper and scrutinized it closely.

'I can't read the text, sir, but this looks like a microfilm press cutting. I've seen them in Bromgrove Library. You can get printouts of newspaper articles, digital news and stuff like that.'

The DI's spine stiffened and his chin came up in a semaphore long familiar to his subordinates.

'What was Snell doing with press cuttings?'

'It has to be relevant, sir.' Burton was keen to crack the forensic sudoku. 'He must have been digging dirt on something.'

'*Or someone*,' breathed Markham.

The stale air of Jim Snell's office suddenly felt full of sinister life. As though an exhalation from the caretaker's dismal nocturnal rituals had intertwined itself, vapour-like, with the floating malice of Hope's murderous stalker to produce an evil miasma. For a moment, Markham felt as if he must choke.

Where in God's name was Snell? The keeper of the keys

with his hellish secrets. The guardian of the basement, Hope's underworld.

Hell. The underworld. *Hades*. Unbidden, an image from his schooldays rose to the surface of Markham's mind. Charon the ferryman, the foul haggard old man tasked with carrying the souls of the dead across the river Styx, his oar brandished over the depths ready to bludgeon any stragglers.

Water.

Markham was later unable to explain the lightning flashes which had shot across his mental landscape leading him to the cistern in the school's huge cobwebby boiler room.

'A tank. Somewhere in the basement.'

Frantically, with shaking hands, he rifled through the innumerable keys on the caretaker's chaotic desk.

'Let me, sir.' Quietly, competently, Burton took over.

After what seemed like an eternity, she detached an item from the jumble.

'This one says Utility Room.'

'Right, let's go!' Markham smashed his fist into his palm. 'If Snell had only come to me first, I could have saved the stupid bastard.'

They located the utility room with surprising ease.

There, in the far right corner was a vast, rusting cistern. About the size of a human body.

A long pole with a hook at its end was propped against the tank. The predator's claw. Markham knew then what they were going to find.

The vat had no lid. A hummock of floating slurry showed, long and narrow like the swelling of a grave mound. The stench of decomposition was unmistakable.

Markham grasped the pole, shoving and prodding at the filthy broth. Sweat streamed down his face as he thrust again and again. Snatching up some abandoned copper pulls, Noakes and Doyle rushed to help, grunting and panting with their exertions.

Burton gasped in horror as the dead caretaker's face appeared, followed slowly by the rest of his body. Snell's pathetic corpse, its face horribly distorted, the mouth agape in an O of terror, floated on a sea of scum. Like a victim of the rack, his limbs were wrenched out of position. Later, behind closed eyelids, the sight haunted the DC's sleep: Snell endlessly rupturing his frogspawn sheath like an avenging spectre.

Markham was close to collapse. Dropping the pole, he fell to his knees. In lieu of a prayer, from somewhere deep within, he dredged up the words of a Psalm: '"My strength is gone, like water poured out onto the ground, and my bones are out of joint. My heart is like wax; it has melted inside me."' Mentally reciting this fragment from a long-forgotten Good Friday service, he felt ineffable sadness as he contemplated all that was left of Jim Snell.

In the aftermath of the discovery, the DI felt mysteriously detached from his surroundings, as though insulated from reality by an invisible wall of plexiglass.

While in this dreamlike state, a kaleidoscope of images flashed across his retina like flickering scenes from a zoetrope.

Snell's body being winched from the cistern with a sickening glutinous whoosh, slithering onto the waiting stretcher in its ghastly amniotic sac.

The soapy yellow-green waxiness of the caretaker's hideously contorted features. The glaucous eyes staring at some invisible horror. The disjointed limbs hanging uselessly like broken hinges.

Markham recalled Matthew Sullivan's epitaph to Audrey Burke. 'She had a life, maybe not a great one, but it was taken away from her.'

Jim Snell might have been the embittered husk of a man, scrabbling in the embers of a half-lived existence, but to die like this...! Racked with shudders, Markham was only dimly aware of a blanket being wrapped around his shoulders.

A concerned face swam into focus. Burton.

'Sir, let's get out of this horrible place. You need tea and lots of sugar, for the shock.'

Noakes and Doyle joined her, having supervised the removal of Snell's remains in their viscous paste (Markham had no recollection of summoning the emergency services). Both looked badly shaken.

Time to lead. Knowing that he had to offer a stable focal point, Markham shrugged off the blanket and made a herculean effort.

'Back to the office. We can regroup there.'

With one last fearful glance around what for him was now a chamber of horrors, Markham led his team out of the boiler room.

12

The Net Tightens

THE MORNING AFTER THE discovery of Jim Snell's body saw Hope Academy closed to students and staff alike. A notice on the school website proclaimed the commencement of half term a day early due to 'a tragic development connected with the police investigation', while two uniforms were posted at the car park gates to deter rubberneckers and the press.

DCI Sidney's reaction had, predictably, been little short of apoplectic, though Markham managed to buy the team some time by dangling the bait of 'a promising line of inquiry connected with the wider community'. Privately, he was convinced that the latest trail would lead inexorably back to Hope, but in the meantime had no scruples about engaging in smoke and mirrors. If implying a connection with local whackjobs got the DCI off his back, then so be it. With Sidney happy to authorize overtime for an expansion of the investigation to include the Newman Hospital and various psychiatric outpatient facilities – this being heavily trailed on local news programmes – Markham got his hastily assembled task force underway taking statements and collecting evidence. Aware that each PC secretly hoped the case might be a stepping stone to promotion and a career in CID, he felt guilty at marching his eager young recruits down a blind alley. But with Sidney to pacify, there was no option but to give a convincing impression that he was bowing to the DCI's superior wisdom.

Burton's interview with Matthew Sullivan had yielded nothing tangible. The drama teacher simply admitted an infatuation with Ashley Dean, confirming that his feelings were unreciprocated and that it ended badly.

'I got the feeling he was holding out on me, sir.' Burton had been unsatisfied with the outcome. 'As though he was protecting someone. But, whatever it was, I couldn't get him to open up.'

Markham wondered if Olivia might have had more success with Sullivan. But he wasn't prepared to risk her safety. As things stood, Sullivan was an unknown quantity with a motive for murder.

Then there was JP. Markham understood the head was due to attend Audrey Burke's funeral at the Methodist Church in Charnley Road later that morning. There would be an opportunity for watching his behaviour and catching him with his guard down. Assuming, that is, he could prise Palmer away from Helen Kavanagh who would no doubt stick to him like superglue.

'I want you to get down to Bromgrove Library,' the DI instructed Noakes and Burton.

'I'm a member, sir,' Burton informed him proudly.

Markham carefully avoided catching Noakes's eye.

'That's excellent, Kate. You and Noakes can check out the archives.'

'What're we looking for, Guv?'

The DS sounded less than enthralled by their assignment.

'Anything to do with Hope.' Markham paused. 'Or other schools in Bromgrove, for that matter.'

He ticked them off on his fingers. 'Bromgrove Secondary, Charnley Technical College, Cothill House, Ferndean, The Elton Partnership... Stick with the secondaries for now – state and independent – and go back a couple of decades.'

The DI raked a hand through the dark hair that was starting to curl below his collar. It gave him a faintly piratical air that struck an incongruous note against the sharp lines of his impeccably cut pinstriped suit.

'Jim Snell *had* something on the murderer. *Knew* something about him.'

Something nasty in the woodshed.

'What sort of thing?' Noakes asked phlegmatically.

Markham lifted his hand deprecatingly. 'Some scandal or secret. That press cutting you found in his office suggests he went to the trouble of doing research.' His face darkened. 'Maybe Audrey knew the secret too.'

'So, Snell was a blackmailer, sir?' Burton's tone was bleak.

'Yes, Kate. I think he intended to trade his knowledge for silence. Provided the price was right.' Markham shivered as if a rabbit had run over his grave. 'The poor fool thought he was in the driving seat ... had no idea what he was up against ...'

For a moment, he stood lost in thought, overwhelmed with revulsion for his job and filled with a longing for Olivia which was almost painful in its intensity. In that dark subterranean world where he toiled like some accursed troglodyte, condemned to sift through the vices and passions of mankind, Olivia was a beacon. All the rest just degradation and damnation.

He became aware that Doyle was speaking.

'... maybe Audrey saw something and clocked it as suspicious. She could've let something slip to Snell ...'

Markham gave himself a mental shake.

'That's more than likely what happened, Constable,' he said approvingly.

The tall gangly PC hopped from one foot to the other in gratification. Like a little kid wanting to spend a penny, thought Noakes disapprovingly.

'Snell was a hate-filled pygmy,' Markham declared. 'He hoarded gossip and secrets. Seized hold of anything scandalous and jumped on it.'

Navigating Hope's murky slipstreams like a crocodile. Until he met his leviathan.

'He was a horrible man, but he didn't deserve to end up like that.' Burton's eyes were suspiciously bright.

'No, he didn't, Kate.' Markham's voice was very gentle.

There was a brief silence, before he resumed in a tone of grim resolution.

'The killer's unravelling. Snell was tortured and Audrey ended up stuffed down the back of a piano. Whatever void Ashley Dean's murder was designed to fill, the act itself was a downer. He – or she – *needed* to kill again. We've got ourselves a serial and we're running out of time. I give it forty-eight hours tops before the DCI's back on the blower threatening to hand this one over to Mr Nicely-Nicely.'

The gloom on the others' faces deepened at this caustic allusion to Superintendent Bretherton, or 'blethering Bretherton' as he was more popularly known.

'Doyle.'

The PC practically clicked his heels.

'You're with me. We'll pay our respects to Audrey and see if anything useful comes our way from JP and Kavanagh. There's bound to be other staff there as well, so we can take a closer look at Uttley, Sullivan and the rest of them while we're about it. The killer has to be suffering a reaction after Snell ... the strain of Audrey's funeral could bring it all to the surface.'

Noakes looked as if he wished he could swap assignments.

'Er, libraries aren't really my bag, Guv,' he ventured.

'High time you expanded your horizons then,' the DI responded with the ghost of a smile as he followed Doyle to the door.

Despite himself, Noakes was rather taken with Bromgrove Library, an imposing colonnaded Victorian building in the town centre.

Burton, of course, was oohing and aahing over everything like some silly sixth former on a day out. Typical snowflake.

Determined not to appear impressed, the DS nevertheless fell under the spell of the main reading room. The place was like something out of a fairy tale, he thought, taking in its circular interior with the domed ceiling and wrought iron spiral staircases leading to rows and rows of old oak shelves. Just seeing the regiments of books lined up behind gilt balustrades gave him a feeling of veneration for learning. Looking round at all the silent scholars hunched over vast tomes under a huge ormolu clock, it was all vast and echoey, like being in church. You'd be afraid to blow your nose in case the sound disturbed someone.

It was with a feeling of some disappointment, therefore, that Noakes followed Burton through the reading room to an undistinguished linoleum-floored modern complex signposted *Local Records* whose airlessness, the DC explained earnestly, was down to the archives needing to be temperature-controlled. Like sodding Center Parcs, he thought crossly.

His stomach gave a rumble.

''Appen I can leave you to get started,' he said with his best winning manner, observing the way his colleague was rapturously drinking in her surroundings. 'There's a Costa Coffee back there an' I missed out on elevenses.'

'OK,' came the surprisingly amiable response. 'I'll ask Miss Todd to set us up on the microfilm readers.' Burton gestured to a desiccated looking woman with cropped hair and a dreary plaid skirt who was eyeing them with a gimlet stare.

'You do that, luv,' he said effusively. 'I'll be back in a tick. Once I've fired up the old carburettor.'

With any luck Miss Congeniality over there would give them a hand. She looked the upright citizen type. In the meantime, he'd have a cuppa. They'd likely be here most of the day and the DI wouldn't want him going under for want of sustenance. Maybe there'd be time for another peep at that reading room too. Just cos he hadn't been to college didn't mean he couldn't appreciate the finer things in life.

Noakes sidled towards the door.

'Glad you could join us, Sergeant,' said Miss Todd on

Noakes's return some three quarters of an hour later. She sounded distinctly nettled.

Time to pour oil on troubled waters.

'Lost track of time looking round the reading room, luv. Hadn't realized it was such a treasure trove. That History of Magic display's champion.'

Bingo. The battle-axe bestowed an approving smile upon him.

'Well, our younger visitors were always commenting that the architecture reminded them of Harry Potter, so it seemed appropriate to offer something about local traditions and tales from the past. We'll be doing Food Through the Ages next.'

'Right up your street, Sarge,' Burton observed with a knowing look.

Noakes hastily changed the subject.

'How's it going with the trawl, then?' he enquired, gesturing at a pile of printouts.

Burton wrinkled her nose.

'Thanks to Miss Todd's indexing skills, better than I'd hoped.'

The librarian retreated to a discreet distance, clearly well pleased with this encomium.

Lowering her voice, Burton continued, 'I'm pulling any school stuff that sounds vaguely juicy – sacked teachers, staff on the fiddle, cheating, bullying … whatever dirt I can dig up, basically.'

Noakes looked warily at the microfilm reader next to Burton's. Following his glance, the DC grinned.

'Nah, Sarge, I'll be quicker doing it myself. But why don't you have a look through the printouts – see if anything jumps out. You've got more local knowledge, so you'll likely join the dots quicker than me.'

'Fair enough.' Noakes assumed an attitude of poker-faced impenetrability, as befitted a custodian of community secrets. Settling his ample buttocks on a low-slung leather chair to the side of the microfilm readers, he began to scan the pile of perforated sheets.

For a while, silence reigned in their corner of the room, broken only by the soft whirr of microfilm reels and an intermittent juddering of the printer. From time to time, Burton cast an amused glance at Noakes who, increasingly absorbed in his task, looked for all the world like an earnest amateur historian.

'Lift a few stones and you wouldn't believe what crawls out.'

The DS sounded genuinely outraged.

'If it's not pervy teachers screwing around with students, it's kids dealing drugs or topping themselves cos of bullying,' he sputtered. 'All I can say is I'm glad my Natalie's done with education.'

Noticing Miss Todd's sudden air of alert attention, he lowered his voice a fraction.

'Seriously, though, it makes you think. My schooldays were like something out of Enid Blyton compared with this lot.'

Despite the attempt at nonchalance, it sounded curiously like a cry for help.

'Maybe if they focused on the three Rs instead of fannying around with all this trendy nonsense ...' the DS grouched, gesturing impotently with the sheaf of papers.

'Too late to stuff that genie back in the bottle, Sarge.'

Burton spoke mildly, surprised to feel an unexpected spasm of pity for her cantankerous colleague under whose feet the tectonic plates were shifting.

The DC leaned back in her chair, trying to ignore the nagging ache in her lower back.

'Anything in particular grab you?' she enquired.

'Well, there's a couple of stories about bullying at Cothill,' Noakes replied, thumbing through the stash. 'I noticed them cos me an' the missus almost sent Natalie there. Went to Open Day an' all.' He looked belligerently at Burton as though daring her to challenge this. 'We could afford it,' he continued defensively, 'but it just didn't feel right. Very swanky, but the kids were right snotty an' the head ... well, he was a real poser ... megawatt smile – the mums loved it – but dead insincere underneath.' He clenched his jaw. 'I caught him sneering at Muriel when he thought she couldn't see. But *I* saw him. I don't mind anyone having a pop at me, but *no-one* laughs at my missus.'

Noakes should have sounded ridiculous but somehow didn't. Seeing only respectful sympathy in Burton's face, he added more temperately, 'One of the stories about Cothill says there was a seventeen-year-old student who killed himself. Single-parent family an' the kid was there on a scholarship. It was down to bullying. The lad left a diary an' it all came out. The form tutor turned a blind eye, apparently.'

'What happened?'

'Oh, there was an investigation but the school decided no-one was to blame.'

'Very convenient.'

'Yeah. But get this,' Noakes's voice swelled with admiration, 'the lad's mum wasn't having any of it. Got up at the inquest and called the form tutor a douchebag. Really went for the whole lot of 'em, the poor cow. Said that if the head wasn't so busy ass-kissing, he'd have noticed what was going on.'

'Good for her.' Burton knew which side she was on. 'When did all this happen?'

'About fifteen years or so. There was a follow up when the mum died suddenly. A relative told the *Gazette* she died of a broken heart an' the staff at Cothill had blood on their hands.'

'God, how awful.' Burton's face looked pinched and drawn at the grim recital.

'Yeah.' Noakes nodded solemnly. 'Ferndean's pretty gross too. Three teachers struck off in the last five years for,' he air quoted savagely, 'inappropriate relationships. An' before that there was a hoo-ha about the head having it off with one of the governors. Turned out he'd been giving her money out of school funds. An' that's not all—'

Burton interrupted before Noakes could embark on a litany of iniquities.

'Anything in there about Hope, Sarge?'

Like a witch-finder baulked of his prey, Noakes abandoned the indictment against Ferndean with some reluctance.

'Nowt to speak of,' he replied. 'Just summat about when an exams officer lost a set of GCSE papers an' the parents were creating about it.'

Burton's eyes throbbed with squinting at microfilm slides. A blinding headache was just around the corner.

'C'mon,' she said wearily. 'I'll just do this last batch. Miss Todd said she'll run some checks too if we don't get finished today.'

Noakes's nose was already deep in the pile of printouts. At some level, reflected Burton, she and the DS had bonded over their abortive *auto-da-fé*.

Perhaps, she concluded with a rueful smile, that was precisely what Markham had intended.

By five o'clock, the team had reconvened in their office at Hope. Outside it was getting dark, a chill wind wuthering mournfully around the building.

The DI looked all done in, Noakes thought as he watched his guv'nor from over the rim of an outsize Bart Simpson mug. Burton was wolfing nurofen tablets like smarties, while Doyle flicked desultorily through a notebook between picking his blackheads.

Markham was recalling Audrey's funeral service. Crenellated and gothic from the outside, the church's long narrow interior was cheerless as a barn with just one stained glass window at the far end. A vaulted ceiling in lurid vermilion, crisscrossed with white rafters, failed to suggest celestial realms to Markham, being more evocative of hell fire.

Unlike the huge turnout for Ashley Dean, the congregation for Audrey had comprised a dispiriting huddle in the front three pews. And of these, most appeared to be her colleagues from Hope. It was so cold that their breath hung in the air.

Matthew Sullivan had held aloof from Markham, but the DI noted that Harry Mountfield appeared to be propping him up. The drama teacher's eyes seemed to look inward at some private agony, so that it felt like a violation to spy on him.

JP's appearance too seemed testament to some deep-seated anguish, his eyes bloodshot behind the heavy black-rimmed spectacles and the scrawny body more tadpole-like than ever. The number two haircut was dank with sweat and an ill-fitting *Man at C&A* suit failed to disguise the fact that he had lost an alarming amount of weight. Was it grief or remorse that had wreaked such havoc on the man, Markham wondered. Helen Kavanagh shadowed Palmer like a prison warder, leaving no opportunity for conversation after the service. Depressingly, the rubicund officiating clergyman referred to Audrey as 'Anne' throughout, delivering a boiler-plate address which served only to highlight the tenuousness of the connection between minister and congregation.

Markham and Olivia, attended by Doyle, both followed the little cortege to Bromgrove South Crematorium, a tiny mouse-hole of a building which somehow suited the inoffensive character of the deceased. Their bouquet of violets was one of just two floral tributes.

As the still, silent coffin inched towards the archway which led to the furnace and the chimney, Markham bowed his head. *I'm so sorry, Audrey*, he said over and over, *I'm so sorry*.

There was no wake. After dropping Olivia back at The Sweepstakes, Markham and Doyle proceeded to the Newman and an endless round of interviews.

Pointless. All utterly pointless. But enough to keep the gold braid mob at bay.

Markham dragged himself back to the present.

'Anything useful in the archives, Noakes?'

'Burton did well, Guv,' came the gruff response.

The DI's lips quirked disbelievingly at this indication of détente, but all he said was, 'Go on.'

'Well, she got most of the school stuff out of the library database or watchamacallit.'

'*Excellent.*'

'We've picked out a selection of articles for you, sir.' Burton took over, her headache forgotten. 'The biggest headlines from the last twenty years or so.'

She handed Markham a sheaf of papers with sections highlighted in different colours.

As she did so, he felt something like a swift electric shock.

The DC looked up at him wonderingly.

'We're going to stop this evil in its tracks,' he said. 'I want you to go home now. But be ready to meet here tomorrow at eight o'clock sharp. I'm going to look at these archive records tonight, and we'll review them tomorrow. It's half term next week, so no students underfoot, but staff will be in and out from Monday. We've got the weekend to come up with something.'

Nothing loath, Burton and Doyle headed for the car park.

'You too, Noakesy,' Markham urged when the DS seemed inclined to linger. 'How do you think Burton's shaping up?' he could not resist asking.

'She's not totally useless,' came the rejoinder as Noakes shuffled on his disreputable parka. 'Got a good head on her shoulders once you get past all that university nonsense.'

It was the flag of truce.

As he switched off lights and locked doors, Markham was at once struck by the building's eerie silence. Previously, even in the absence of Hope's students, there had been a background hum – the bustle of the scholastic anthill. Now that was hushed as if it had never been.

This hinterland had been Jim Snell's world.

Until the golem came for him.

Markham strode for the foyer without looking back, fingering his bundle of papers as though it was a talisman.

This is it, he told himself. The last throw of the dice.

13

Shadows from the Past

'SO FINALLY, IT'S PEACE in our time!'

Markham chuckled reminiscently as he described the rapprochement between Noakes and Kate Burton.

By tacit consent, he and Olivia had shelved the subject of the investigation during supper, talking in a desultory fashion about other things, though with a burning consciousness of the press cuttings in Markham's study.

'Well, I know you can't do without Noakes,' Olivia remarked indulgently, 'and I've always had a soft spot for him, though he's a strange mixture ... childlike, cunning and comforting all at once.'

'Burton likely dismissed him out of hand as an uncouth philistine. And God knows the old villain plays up to that image for all he's worth. But he's full of surprises.' He laughed again. 'D'you know he's a leading light of the Silhouette Ballroom Club?'

'*Noakes!*'

'The very same. Heard it at the gym from another DI. Apparently, he's a demon on the dance floor.'

'Now that *would* be worth seeing.' Olivia's eyes sparkled with mischief. 'Can you imagine him and Muriel doing the paso doble?'

'Oh, she got him into it, apparently. They're regulars on the exhibition circuit. Take it very seriously.'

'Well, just when you think you know someone ...'

A shadow fell across Olivia's face at the thought that there might be someone close at hand whom she had never truly known at all. A lost soul. Like a dark continent – one of those huge desolate tracts on ancient maps of the world that medievalists inscribed with the words *Hic Sunt Dracones*. Here be dragons.

Catching sight of his girlfriend's expression, Markham said, 'We're very close now, Liv, I can feel it.' Pouring himself another cup of coffee, he added urgently, 'I can't shake the feeling that we're on the edge of a breakthrough. When Burton gave me those press cuttings, I had this superstitious feeling that the key to the case lay right there, buried somewhere amongst all the headlines and gossip.'

'Time to find out, then!' Olivia met his eyes bravely. 'May I go through them with you? *Please, Gil.* Another pair of eyes and all that.'

'Of course. Let's take our drinks through to the study.'

In Markham's study, Olivia hastily closed the curtains against the darkness, as though to barricade the room against night-time demons. Switching on the anglepoise lamp on the desk, and drawing up a second chair, she solemnly divided the press cuttings between them. Side by side in silence, they perused headlines, sidebars and articles for anything that seemed just a hair off-centre.

'Oh, I've found the story you said Noakes was up in arms about,' Olivia announced after a quarter of an hour's careful inspection.

'Which one was that?' Markham enquired absently.

'That one about Cothill House. Noakes said he'd been thinking about it for Natalie but didn't like the way the head poked fun at Muriel, remember?'

'Oh, yes. Wasn't there something about bullying and a suicide?'

Suddenly, Olivia snatched up the printout and studied it intently. 'My goodness, *there's Harry Mountfield!*' She squinted doubtfully and then said, 'No, I must have got it wrong – different name – but it looks awfully like him ... could almost be his twin.'

Markham felt as though blood vessels had burst and flooded into his brain.

He kept his voice steady.

'Show me, Liv.'

'It's a really grainy photo. The sixth form are at the top with the littlies at the front.'

She slid her finger along the paper.

'There's the poor boy who killed himself, second from the left on the next to back row. His brother's on the very back row, the lad on the end ... he's so like Harry, that for moment I thought ... The kid who died was in the lower sixth ... Adrian Medlock ... he had a non-identical twin brother ... let's see ... Howard. So, no connection. Just a weird coincidence.'

Olivia was struck by Markham's unnatural stillness and

the sudden haggardness of his face.

'What is it, Gil?' Then, more urgently, 'Why are you looking like that?'

'Oh, Liv,' came the reply, barely above a hoarse whisper. '*I think you know.*'

The colour drained from Olivia's face, leaving her like the ghost of herself.

'No,' she breathed. 'It can't be.'

Automatically, she reached for Markham's hand. It was there waiting, and as the strong fingers closed on hers, she found the willpower to say one word through clenched teeth.

'Harry.'

With gentle inexorability, Markham confirmed, 'Yes, Harry.'

Olivia felt as though the fragile cocoon that she was weaving around herself had been brutally torn open, leaving a desperate little moth struggling for life inside. Nevertheless, she looked trustfully at her lover and tightened her clasp on his hand.

Markham spoke with quiet seriousness, reaching for another printout emblazoned with the headline *Tragic mum dies of broken heart.*

'It says that after Adrian's death, his mother got involved with groups for survivors of child sexual abuse. At the inquest, before the coroner shut her down, she talked about Cothill being a "perverts' paradise".'

'Mothers just *know* when something's wrong, don't they?'

Not all mothers, Markham thought sadly as he recalled the abuse that had blighted his own childhood and the parent who looked the other way.

Aloud, he said, 'If there was something dodgy about Cothill, Adrian's mum might have *felt* it without being sure. Maybe she only put two and two together after the poor boy died and his diary came to light. It just says here that he had suffered bullying of a sexual nature and suggests staff protected and may even have encouraged the bullies.'

Anger blazed through Markham, but his voice remained even.

'Clearly there was a cover up. This was fifteen years ago. It couldn't be buried in the same way today.'

'But how ...'

Olivia's bewildered, stricken face pleaded for answers.

'What was it people said about Jimmy Savile – something about him hiding in plain sight? That poor boy's family probably felt staff at Cothill were doing the same.'

Markham stood up, walked across to the window and threw back the curtains, looking out into the darkness as though throwing down a gauntlet to the forces of evil.

Then he turned back to Olivia.

'It was the twin brother Howard who accused Adrian's teachers of having blood on their hands.'

The older brother.

It will have blood. Blood will have blood.

'I think we'll find that JP was one of the teachers at Cothill,' Markham said slowly, 'probably Adrian's form tutor.'

'But how did Harry ... I mean Howard ... ever come to be at Hope?'

'It's been staring us in the face all along, Liv! Someone who's waited all this time in the shadows. Someone who was just a young man when his brother died. Someone who reinvented himself then bided his time. And all the while he had James Palmer in his crosshairs.'

'Why would JP give ... Howard ... a job at Hope if he knew who he really was?' It was too much for Olivia to take in.

'*Guilt*, Liv, *guilt*. Plus, Howard knew all about JP and Cothill. No way did Palmer want the governors getting wind of that.'

'Where did Ashley fit into it?'

'JP had fallen in love with Ashley. Howard planned to kill the man Palmer loved and lay his life waste. Then frame him for Dean's murder.'

'But it all went wrong ... Audrey ...'

'Yes, Audrey.' Markham's face twisted. 'She must've seen or suspected something. That first day at the Learning Resource Centre, she didn't want to go in, seemed frightened of someone who was already inside. Harry Mountfield.'

'So, Audrey tried to blackmail him then?'

'Who can say? Maybe the poor woman actually *sympathized* with Mountfield. If she got wind of how Ashley had made her a laughing stock, she wouldn't have been sorry to see the back of him. She was religious, so maybe she was able to square her conscience by coming up with some plan for Mountfield to make amends ...'

'What about Jim Snell?'

'Audrey could've let something slip. Or maybe Mountfield got careless. The strain must have been immense. His exquisite revenge, that he had been incubating for so many years, suddenly derailing before his eyes.'

Markham joined Olivia back at the desk, slipping an arm around her shoulders.

'There was a part of Harry Mountfield that people didn't know. But the Harry *you* knew as your good friend, he also existed, Liv. No-one can take that away from you.'

'I still can't take it in, Gil. Are you *sure*?' Olivia stammered. 'I mean, our Harry ... the joker, the gentle giant ... did *that*?'

'Yes, dearest, I'm sure.' Markham's voice rang with conviction. 'I think we'll find that as a young man he had unresolved homosexual leanings. What happened to Adrian turned all his impulses inwards so that they festered and became deformed. When he mutilated Ashley Dean, I think at some level he was trying to obliterate himself.'

Olivia's eyes shimmered with tears.

'How horrible.' She was clearly grieving for the man she had never really known. 'What're you going to do, Gil?'

'Nothing tonight. I'm briefing the team first thing tomorrow. We'll draw up a plan to bring him in ... He thinks we're looking at JP and Sullivan—'

'Oh God, yes.' Olivia's gentle nature was roused. 'How *could* he let Matt fall under suspicion?'

'Well, he planted that letter designed to steer us in the direction of JP – the unsigned one we found in Ashley's locker divulging Palmer's feelings for him. It wasn't part of his plan to implicate Sullivan.'

Olivia began to shake, her skin a sudden rash of goosebumps.

'I'm going to fetch you a brandy,' Markham declared. 'For the shock. And then we're going to turn in. You've had enough for one night.'

Outside in the darkness, the wind had picked up, its

relentless susurration an ominous murmur.

To Olivia's ears, it seemed the agonized moan of a soul in torment.

'*Harry Mountfield*! You've got to be joking, Guv!'

Noakes stared at the DI in lumpen perplexity. Burton and Doyle, meanwhile, stood as though turned to stone.

'Lemme get this clear, Guv. You're figuring *Mountfield* for the murderer. But he's a straight up bloke, for God's sake. Just about the only genuine character in the whole place ... 'cept your Olivia and that funny old geezer in the batman getup.'

Noakes found support in an unexpected quarter.

'Are you quite sure, sir?'

Kate Burton's tone was respectful but troubled.

'You said Mountfield and Sullivan were the good guys, sir. "On the side of the angels" was how you put it.'

Noakes was swaying like a mortally wounded rhino.

'She's right, boss. Mountfield's a total softie. You *saw* how he was with spacey Jakey an' those other kids. How could he fake that? An' he's practically one of us. Scored the winning goal for our lads against the Pendleby Pistols.'

The DI looked at Noakes compassionately.

'Sit down, Noakesy.'

He turned to Burton.

'Check with the uniforms on reception that the building is completely clear. And tell them *no-one in or out except on my express say-so.*'

Burton was out of the door almost before he had finished speaking.

'Doyle, you get the teas in. Well sugared.'

The young PC hastened to obey, casting a wary glance at the DS. But, for once, there was no running commentary on 'people with two left feet'. Noakes sat as though stunned.

On Burton's return, Markham explained his discoveries of the previous night.

Doyle scratched his five o'clock shadow in bemusement.

'Is Mountfield – or Medlock, or whoever he is – a phoney, then? Not a real teacher?'

'I've no doubt his qualifications are the real deal.' Markham was crisply authoritative. 'A bright articulate bloke like that. It was the perfect career. The perfect cover story. *Hiding in plain sight.*'

'How could Mountfield bottle everything up for so long?' Burton wondered.

'He kept it all inside, stoking his hate.'

Markham was soberly matter of fact.

'He must have gloated over the punishment he planned to inflict on Ashley and JP. It was the only way to cauterize the appalling guilt he felt for having failed his vulnerable brother—'

'Adrian's death wasn't his fault,' Burton interjected.

'The tragedy happened when he was an adolescent,' the DI pointed out. 'A difficult age. At some level, he blamed himself for the way his little family went smash. And if he was conflicted about his sexuality, that would have compounded the guilt. Nowadays he'd be whisked in for counselling and what have you, but fifteen years ago ...' Markham raised both palms in a gesture of despairing futility.

Noakes was still shaking his head.

'But Mountfield's nothing like a gay bloke, Guv.'

'I think you'll find there's no e-fit in such cases, Noakes.'

'But look at him an' your Olivia. They're *like that.* Best mates an' all!'

The DS crossed his chipolata fingers and waved them in front of Markham for emphasis. 'Been friends for donkey's years, haven't they?'

The sadness in Markham's face was more eloquent than any words.

Noakes subsided into wretched silence, looking at the DI like a forlorn child.

'The man passing himself off as Harry Mountfield is a chameleon, Noakes. That's what makes him exceptionally dangerous. Olivia never suspected any of this for a moment.'

'Did you never have an inkling, sir?'

There was no impertinence in Burton's enquiry, just a grave curiosity.

'Hindsight's a marvellous thing, Kate.' Markham addressed her as an equal. 'I did very briefly wonder … it was when I was talking to Helen Kavanagh about the letter we found in Ashley's locker – the one which purported to come from Palmer.'

'What happened?' Noakes's lethargy was forgotten, his expression eager.

'Nothing specific. But our man was there in the room with Helen Kavanagh when we were talking about it. I said the letter could have been planted to frame Palmer and he said it would take powerful hatred to do something like that.'

'Is that all?' The DS sounded disappointed.

'Not quite. When I replied that it could be hatred or love,

because they were two sides of the same coin, he gave me a peculiar look. I didn't interpret it correctly at the time. But now I realize he was applying those words to himself. He hated JP and Ashley, but maybe at another level he was obsessed with them too … maybe half in love with one or the other, or both.'

'Creepy,' said Doyle with feeling. Markham could tell he was winning them over.

'Then there was the first day of the investigation,' continued Markham. 'When I was standing outside with him looking at the tributes to Ashley, there was something disturbing – almost avid – about the way he stared at them and watched JP.' He looked round at the team. 'I hold my hands up,' he said quietly. 'There were signals I should have picked up on but didn't.'

Had over-reliance on Olivia's judgement prevented him from seeing Lucifer lurking beneath Harry Mountfield's bonhomie? Had his relish for her wit and candour prevented him from seeing the bigger picture? Had Audrey Burke and Jim Snell died because he had been a blind fool?

'Don't, sir.' Burton broke in upon the tumult of his thoughts.

'Don't what?' Markham could barely trust himself to speak.

'Don't beat yourself up, sir. If Audrey had come to us, she'd be alive. But she was obsessed with Palmer, remember. Probably thought she could protect JP by doing a deal with Mountfield.'

'She's right, Guv. Audrey wasn't going to open up for any of us. Even Tracey Roach said she hadn't twigged that something was bothering her.'

Burton shot Noakes a grateful look.

Doyle chipped in. 'Jim Snell was hell bent on going it alone too, sir.'

'Probably getting off on it,' commented Noakes sagely. 'Imagined he was pulling the strings. One in the eye to everyone who'd written him off as Hope's resident saddo.'

'I dismissed Snell as a pathetic crawler. Audrey too. When all the time ...'

Markham recalled Harry Mountfield's hulking leonine radiance and maverick charm.

'He was a split personality, sir.' Once again Burton demonstrated her uncanny ability to read his thoughts. 'It was the only way he could survive. Part of him must've somehow closed off after what happened to Adrian – functioning normally as far as anyone could tell, but all the anger buried deep inside.'

Like a man being pursued by the Furies, Markham silently added. In a sudden flash of insight, he saw how Mountfield's malice could become omnivorous, insatiable; how he must secretly have craved revenge upon those who were gloriously whole, not maimed as he was.

Noakes was becoming uncomfortable with the psychoanalysis.

'Mountfield's an evil bastard, end of. Next thing you'll be saying he didn't get enough cuddles when he was little or some other bullshit excuse.'

It was authentic Noakes. Clearly the DS was staging a recovery.

'I'm just saying nothing's straightforward here.' Burton was emollient. 'I think Mountfield's sick. Maybe he even *wants* to be caught. Like he knows that the Harry Mountfield who took over Howard Medlock has to be done away with.'

The other grunted.

For an instant Markham felt envious of Noakes's blissfully uncomplicated world view. The narrative of the human spirit was to him a script easily perused rather than a mysterious palimpsest.

'What do you want us to do, Guv?'

Noakes was back where Markham needed him. Four square behind his guv'nor.

'The man we know as Harry Mountfield – in reality Howard Medlock – has no idea we're onto him. I want discreet surveillance on him right away. Palmer too.'

'D'you think JP knows the score, sir?'

'Oh yes, Kate. I think that's what he meant when Noakes and I overheard him raving to Kavanagh that it was a nightmare and there was no way out. He knows who the killer is all right. Must be crucified by guilt that Ashley died because of what happened all those years ago in another life.'

'What about Kavanagh?'

'I'm not sure how much she knows, Noakes. She said to JP, "He played you", remember? She could have meant Ashley Dean or Mountfield.'

'Maybe Kavanagh made it clear to Palmer that she didn't want to hear the specifics – so she'd have deniability.' Burton's mind was racing. 'Maybe she thinks it's something to do with Matthew Sullivan or some sort of homosexual love triangle.'

'Anything's possible.' Markham realized he was gripping the sides of his chair so hard that his hands hurt. Consciously, he willed himself to relax.

'The priority is to bring Mountfield in safely. You see, I think he may be decompensating.'

'You mean he's starting to enjoy killing, sir?'

'Exactly that.' Markham's voice was insistent. 'He hadn't even bothered to do a proper trawl of Snell's office, otherwise he'd have disposed of that press cutting.'

'Shouldn't we bring him in right away, sir?' Burton was taut as a bowstring.

'We need a confession, Kate. Something incontrovertible. No room for doubt.'

The words *DCI Sidney* hung unspoken in the air.

The DI rose to his feet and the others followed suit.

'Burton and Doyle, get the surveillance sorted.'

'On it, sir.'

Markham turned to the DS.

'We need to track down Helen Kavanagh. She may know or suspect Mountfield's the killer. Either way, she can give us some sort of inside track to his thinking.'

'I'll bring the car round, Guv.'

Markham remained alone in the little office and bowed his head.

Help me resolve this, he prayed desperately.

The hairs on the back of his neck suddenly rose.

As though Harry Mountfield's victims were in the room, their arms outstretched, begging for justice.

'Not long now,' he promised.

Then he was striding to the door.

14

Nemesis

MARKHAM AND NOAKES SAT in their unmarked squad car outside Helen Kavanagh's address. Cromptons Lane was an undistinguished street of Victorian terraced houses off the motorway leading out of Bromgrove. Tall sycamores lined both sides of the road, their spindly branches splayed in a tangled canopy against the louring sky.

Kate Burton had radioed that all was quiet at Palmer's address, JP having waved his soon-to-be-ex-wife Cheryl off from Calderstones Drive before vanishing indoors. Since then, nothing. Meanwhile, PC Doyle and two other officers in plain clothes were stationed at a discreet distance from Ramleh Villas where the man known as Harry Mountfield had a ground floor apartment. Mountfield had emerged once, but only to buy a newspaper and cigarettes at the corner shop.

Markham should have felt secure, but a hard knot of fear would not let him relax, the very trees seeming to plot against him like conspiring ghosts.

A thin drizzle began to fall, and the October day turned even murkier.

'What's our approach with Cruella, then?' asked Noakes.

Markham winced. That was Mountfield's nickname for Kavanagh, and it had stuck.

'We ask for Kavanagh's help,' he said baldly. 'Tell her what we've got and throw ourselves on her mercy. We need a confession. Maybe she's the one to help us get it.'

Noakes thrust out his underlip as far as it would go, a sure sign of profound scepticism.

Markham grimaced.

'Well, we've got no forensics, have we? Mountfield was very careful to leave no trace of himself anywhere – not even on that letter in Ashley's locker.' He thumped the dashboard sharply in frustration. 'And even if we can make the case for Mountfield's true identity, so what? It doesn't prove he killed any of the three victims. It's a plausible hypothesis, Noakes, but a QC would shred it in court. And the top brass would throw us to the wolves.'

'You think Kavanagh can get us more evidence, Guv?'

'It's possible. Or she may know which buttons to press – how to trigger Mountfield's tipping point. There could be something in what Kate said before about him almost *wanting* to be caught ... Perhaps Howard Medlock, that bright young sixth former with the world before him, knows that the Harry Mountfield who took over has to be destroyed.'

'Sounds like summat out of *Alien*,' scoffed Noakes, but Markham could see that he was thinking hard. 'So Mountfield could be one of them split personality types, then?'

'I'm no psychiatrist, Noakes, but I don't see how he could

have survived otherwise.' The DI continued tentatively. 'It must have taken incredible effort all these years – living like a shadow man, fighting to hold himself together, knowing that one misstep and it could all come apart.'

'Jekyll and Hyde then.'

Noakes never ceased to surprise him.

'Exactly like that.'

The DS jiggled in his seat, having no other outlet for his gratification.

'It's difficult to believe that the façade of good humour and caring that we saw was only that, a thin veneer,' said Markham sadly. 'There could have been – should have been – so much more.'

For a moment, he sat lost in a brown study, thinking of the man whom he had found so engaging from their earliest meeting.

Olivia's friend.

Then he recollected himself.

'Let's go, Noakes.'

Hope's deputy head lived at number 87, a narrow three-storey house in yellow brick – 'lavatory brick', as Markham thought of it.

Casually dressed in jeans, chunky striped slipper socks and oversized jumper, Helen Kavanagh answered the bell so quickly, that Markham thought she must have been watching from behind the thick net curtains.

She ushered them swiftly into a front room that was as dreary as a dentist's waiting area: black leather three-piece suite; deep pile tobacco-colour carpet; potted ferns; a couple of David Hockney prints; small electric fire with an ugly brick cladding surround. A blizzard of files and paperwork over-flowed the long coffee table onto the floor.

Out of her corporate armour, Kavanagh presented a less daunting picture. The pudding bowl fringe swung limply above red eyelids, and blotchy cheeks which showed evidence of recent crying. Scrubbed clean of makeup, with the neglected traces of silent tears, she looked far removed from the home counties harridan who queened it at Hope.

Flicking the switch on the fire to take the chill off the room, she motioned them to sit down, twisting and untwisting her hands as though being inwardly grappled.

'I know why you're here.'

It was a subdued monotone, no trace of the town crier's boom which had previously offended their ears.

'We'd like to hear it from you first, if that's all right.' Markham spoke soothingly, as though pouring ointment over a wound.

Something seemed to click in Kavanagh's throat, like a clock about to strike, but she held their gaze.

'People died at Hope because of JP's fucking midlife crisis.'

The expletive sounded shocking from her lips.

'I saw what Ashley Dean was about and warned JP to be careful, but he took no notice.' She traced a circle on the carpet with her foot. 'Though I suppose if you've been living a lie most of your life, you end up unable to distinguish gold from dross.'

A pause. Again, that curious clicking of the throat.

'Ashley was a scheming opportunist. At first, I figured he must've been murdered by someone on the staff – someone he'd goaded beyond endurance.'

She swallowed hard.

'I know Ashley died because of something in JP's past. JP told me the killer had a hold on him because of something that happened long ago. He didn't give me a name. *And I didn't want to know.*'

Kavanagh looked at the two men with a fierce challenge in her eyes.

'I didn't want to know who it was,' she repeated passionately. 'I just wanted to keep my school safe!' Her voice was a defiant whisper now. 'There isn't anything else.'

Beyond the words stretched acres of loneliness.

Markham waited patiently.

'Then Audrey and Jim Snell died.' Her fringe was damp with sweat. 'And even then, all I could think about was Hope's reputation. I was *desperate, desperate* for you to look elsewhere.' Something in their faces must have struck home, because she added, 'I'm ashamed. Believe me, if I could turn the clock back ...'

Markham spoke simply. 'You left Ashley Dean's murderer free to kill again.'

'Yes, God forgive me, I did.'

She was gulping for air now. Great angry gulps. 'The poor stupid fools. They must have worked it out ...'

'Did *you* work it out, Helen?' Markham asked calmly.

A swift nod. 'It was down to a throwaway comment in the common room. I doubt anyone else even noticed ...'

Nervously, she rubbed her swollen eyes.

'JP was holding forth after his usual fashion. I was only half listening, but then he said "When I was at Cothill". He was looking straight at Harry Mountfield as he said it, then suddenly went bright red and stopped in mid-sentence ... I didn't think much of it at the time, but it was odd and later I remembered. Other things came back to me too. Things which made me wonder if there was some connection between JP and Harry ... before they came to Hope ...'

'What sort of things?'

'Oh, just something in the air whenever they were together ... something intense about the way Harry looked at JP ... and how JP seemed somehow *submissive* around Harry, rarely looked him in the eyes – not at all like the way he behaved with the rest of us.' She thought for a moment. 'I guess that's why that moment in the common room stuck in my mind.'

'Did you ask Palmer about Mountfield?'

'No. It would have been all up with us if I'd done that.' She gave a tremulous laugh. 'It was like we had a secret understanding. Ask me no questions and I'll tell you no lies.'

'What were you planning on doing?' Noakes's voice was harsh with incredulity. 'Were you ever going to put us straight? Or were you hoping to pin it on some fruitcake from the Newman?'

Helen Kavanagh flushed painfully.

They had their answer.

Noakes wouldn't let it go.

'What about the kids? What about your colleagues? You thought it was OK to have a maniac teaching RE? What about "thou shalt not kill", luv?' He was almost shouting now, his face puce with indignation. 'Ring any fucking bells?'

'I'd have found a way of getting Harry away from Hope somehow.'

'Huh! He'd likely have gone for you next.'

The woman turned so pale, that Markham thought she was going to faint. He shot Noakes a warning look.

'We need to bring Harry Mountfield in, Helen. And we need evidence against him. Before anyone else gets hurt.'

'I'd like to help, but ...'

'Any chance you could lure Mountfield into school on some pretext or other and confront him with your suspicions? We'd have you wired up with officers on standby.'

'Won't he smell a rat?'

'It's a risk we'll have to take. Certainly, Palmer's in no fit state for anything of the kind.'

'I'll do it.'

Helen Kavanagh looked earnestly at Markham.

'I've messed up very badly, Inspector. I want to make amends.'

'Good. That takes guts.' The DI spoke sincerely, and a faint pleasure stole over her face.

Suddenly, Noakes's radio crackled into life.

'Something amiss at Calderstones Drive, Guv,' the DS said guardedly.

'Tell Kate we're on our way. We'll be in touch, Helen.'

In a matter of minutes, they were on the road, siren blaring as they raced to respond.

By the time they arrived at number 4 Calderstones Drive, it was raining hard, a driving vertical downpour which drenched the two men as they ran up the front steps where Kate Burton was waiting.

'What is it, Kate?'

'Mrs Lynch from number 6 came out a minute ago.' Burton gestured to the handsome semi-detached property on the other side of the low fence which divided the two houses. 'She kept ringing Palmer's bell but there was no answer. When I asked what was wrong, she said she'd heard a heavy thud which seemed to come from the loft next door ... seemed spooked by it, sir.'

Markham gazed up at number 4. Nothing stirred within its bow-windowed interior.

'There's a spare set of keys, sir. JP left them with Mrs Lynch in case he ever lost his or got locked out.'

'No need to force entry then,' said Markham. 'Right, Kate, you wait here please while Noakes and I check it out.'

All was still and silent, save for the soft hiss of rain and the steady ticking of a grandfather clock from somewhere in the house. Markham led the way up three flights of richly carpeted stairs, arriving finally at a black steel spiral staircase leading to the loft conversion.

'Mr Palmer,' he called softly.

No reply.

At the top of the stairs, the DI saw what, in his heart, he had known would be waiting for them.

JP's grotesquely elongated body oscillating gently beneath a skylight on the far side of the sloping roof, one dangling foot seeming to stretch desperately towards the floor where a chest of drawers lay overturned.

Moving closer, Markham saw the glazed eyes which seemed fixed on the distant sky beyond the skylight. The jaw hung agape and a small stream of froth bubbled from discoloured, purple lips.

'God in Heaven.'

Noakes had his pen knife out and was hacking desperately

at the garden rope secured round the screwjack opener.

'*Come on,*' he muttered frantically. '*Come on.*'

Markham watched as the DS cut down the body and laid it on the ground.

'He's light as a feather,' Noakes whispered. 'Poor bugger.'

Poignantly, JP's spectacles were carefully folded into the top pocket of his sweatshirt. As though he did not wish to see too clearly while the shadows lengthened and the world outside was hushed.

For now we see through a glass, darkly, but then face to face.

Ashley Dean was the god of JP's idolatry, Ashley's the face he looked for at the end.

There was a commotion on the stairs and ragged panting.

Cheryl Palmer burst into the loft, closely followed by Kate Burton.

'I'm sorry, sir,' she gasped. 'I couldn't stop her.'

'It's all right, Kate.'

Markham caught JP's estranged wife in his arms and spun her around, away from the crumpled form on the ground. But not before she had seen the ghastly flaccid face and the thick cord cinched so tightly around her husband's neck that it looked half its normal size.

Struggling fiercely, Cheryl let out an unearthly wail. Then her legs buckled and she fell.

Noakes and Burton rushed to the shrieking woman, between them pulling her to her feet and manoeuvring her down the staircase.

Markham stood rooted to the spot, listening as her anguished screams grew fainter and fainter.

Then he looked down at the pitiful corpse.

At least, he reflected, JP had chosen the manner of his own passing, had been absolute for death and baulked his tormentor of the longed-for vengeance.

Nothing could touch him further.

Light as a feather, Noakes had said.

The DI breathed a silent prayer that in whatever mysterious bourne he now resided, James Palmer was at last free as air.

The rest of the day seemed to pass in a blur.

DCI Sidney, aghast at a suicide connected to Bromgrove's flagship academy, wanted a media blackout. It took all Markham's powers of persuasion to convince him otherwise.

'We now have a firm suspect, sir,' he insisted, 'with every likelihood that the news of Mr Palmer's suicide will bring him into the open.'

The DCI eyed him like a rattlesnake.

'Hope's deputy head has agreed to a covert operation, sir,' Markham continued. 'We're dealing with an individual traumatized by a past family tragedy, and she is a psychologist by training.'

It was a stretch, but the medical eyewash was his best hope. Sidney wanted to keep his cosy relationship with Bromgrove LEA unsullied by any scandalous revelations, so the vaguer the better.

'You've got twenty-four hours,' came the stony response. 'After that, Markham, you're off the case, capeesh?'

'Hearing you loud and clear, sir. And thank you.'

Back in CID, two anxious faces turned to greet him.

'Twenty-four hours or it's over to Bretherton.' The DI's

mouth was bitter, and he snapped his fingers to reinforce the point.

Noakes appeared even more down at heel and dishevelled than usual. Kate Burton, by contrast, looked bandbox fresh and appeared to have changed her shirt. And yet, the two appeared closer than the DI had yet seen them, as though a mysterious connection had secretly flowered underground and was pushing up delicate shoots towards the light.

It might be the only good thing to come out of this damned investigation, he thought savagely.

'Get hold of the press office, Kate. We need a broadcast about JP for the early evening news.'

As she disappeared, Markham turned to Noakes.

'Mountfield'll be monitoring the media – trying to stay three steps ahead,' he said wearily. 'With luck, the news about Palmer will screw him emotionally.'

'What about Helen Kavanagh?'

'Babysitting job. Once this bulletin's in the can, we'll get over there and work on a script.'

'Do you think she can deliver, Guv?'

'Well, she's guilt-stricken over Audrey and Jim Snell. Desperate to atone.'

'Could be a loose cannon.'

'Undoubtedly, but what else have we got?'

There was a reckless light in the DI's eyes. Noakes had seen that look before. It meant Markham had the scent of blood in his nostrils.

'How long do we give Mountfield before Kavanagh asks for a meeting?' The DS was revolving all the variables in his mind.

'A couple of hours.' Markham's speech quickened. 'Look, he'll be completely blindsided. JP's out of it forever. The man this was supposedly all about gone in a flash. Don't forget, those fantasies about revenge have dominated Mountfield's whole life. And now, at a stroke, the plan's in tatters. If ever he needed to unburden himself – free his soul – it's now.'

'An' if he thinks Kavanagh's on to him, he'll have to fix her one way or another ...'

Noakes screwed up his craggy features in profound cogitation. A pause, then, 'You can count on me, Guv.'

Until then, Markham did not realize he had been holding his breath.

'Let's get a drink and something to eat in the canteen, Noakes. After that, we can plan Kavanagh's big reveal.'

An hour later, having polished off fried eggs and beans on toast, all washed down with scalding hot tea, Markham and Noakes were back in Markham's office preparing a crib sheet for Helen Kavanagh.

Kate Burton appeared in the doorway.

'PC Doyle's just radioed in, sir.' Her voice was strained.

'Isn't Doyle outside Mountfield's place with the plainclothes lads we borrowed from Vice?'

'Yes, Sarge. But ...'

Markham heard the note of rising panic.

'What's happened, Kate?'

'He was waiting round the back of Ramleh Villas, near the garages.'

'And?' rumbled Noakes impatiently.

'Well, somehow Mountfield gave him the slip ...'

'Didn't he have the flat in his direct line of sight?'

'Yes, sir. He went around the corner just to stretch his legs. A matter of minutes. When he got back, he noticed the French window was open ...'

'*Oh God.*' Markham's voice was choked.

'What is it, sir?'

The DI's olive complexion had turned ashy pale.

'*Helen Kavanagh.*'

Noakes was on his feet, working it out.

'JP's gone. She's next in line.'

'But Kavanagh didn't have anything to do with his brother's death,' Burton faltered, looking from one to the other.

'Mountfield's beyond making that kind of distinction.' Markham's voice was the merest thread. 'We've flipped his switch all right. He wants a substitute for JP.'

'She won't let him in, will she?'

'I think she will,' the DI replied hoarsely as though debating with himself. 'She said she wanted to make amends.'

Burton reached for her police radio.

'*No!*'

The command came fast as the crack of a whip.

'Sir, he's a madman.'

'If we go in mob-handed, anything could happen.'

Not a fourth victim.

'We do it the guv'nor's way.'

Noakes looked Burton directly in the eye. She nodded and their compact was sealed.

The three officers moved as one towards the door. Ready to confront their nemesis.

15

Cornered

IN THE UNDERGROUND CAR park beneath the station, they found Doyle waiting, his bluff yokel's face the picture of shame and confusion.

'I'm sorry, sir,' he blurted miserably. 'Got itchy feet and thought a quick whiz round the corner'd wake me up like. It was just minutes, but when I got back ...'

'Numpty,' was Noakes's succinct response.

The young PC was clearly crushed at the thought that he might have blown his chances in CID.

'It's all right, Doyle,' said Markham kindly. 'You'd been hanging about for hours. Understandable that you took your eye off the ball for a moment. Could have happened to any of us.'

Not to me, Noakes and Burton thought in unison.

'You're a good officer,' Markham continued as they piled into the squad car. 'The main thing is to learn from this and move on.'

An' stop mooning over that dippy girlfriend. Noakes's expression was eloquent in its disapproval, but he said nothing, merely gestured Doyle to the driver's seat. Markham got in the front next to him, while the other two sat in the back.

'No sirens,' the DI instructed, 'but over to Cromptons Lane as fast as you can, Doyle.'

It was still raining relentlessly, mixed now with hail. Inside the bubble of their car, speeding along in the gathering darkness, Kate Burton felt as though they were the last people alive, marooned in a nightmare, huddled together for protection. Like something out of a sci-fi movie. Only the evil they had to eliminate was no vampire but a flesh and blood human being. Someone whom, until recently, she had seen as one of them.

Markham's thoughts ran in an equally sombre groove. Could he prevent further carnage? What could he offer Harry Mountfield beyond the secure wing of a psychiatric hospital, through whose bars he would be poked and prodded for the rest of his days like a freak of nature? The urbane, witty teacher who could never be healed, whose inner void could never be filled. Always insatiable, always hungry, always lost.

Things bad begun make strong themselves by ill.

The journey towards the motorway seemed interminable, even though the rush hour was long over. The hail persisted with its ominous drumming, as though even the elements were rallying for the final assault.

Finally, they were outside number 87.

There was a figure at the window, silhouetted against lamplight, looking out into the darkness. Then it withdrew into the shadowy recesses of the front room.

Mountfield.

Burton drew in her breath sharply. 'He's here.'

'He didn't run then,' Doyle said wonderingly.

'Where would he go?' asked Markham. 'We'd find him eventually.'

'He could've tried to bluff it out,' observed Noakes meditatively, 'but he must have known the net was closing at Hope. With JP's death, we'd have been all over 'im like a rash and the truth was bound to come out.' The DS pulled a face. ''Sides, he's worked up an appetite now. On a spree, isn't he?'

Burton shuddered, but she realized it was true. Mountfield saw his mission as far from over. His blood lust still demanded satisfaction.

'We go in calmly, quietly. No theatrics, understood?' Markham's voice was peremptory. 'The priority is to get them both out of there alive.'

There would be no chance at all if the place was swarming with tactical support, hostage negotiators, Uncle Tom Cobley and all, he thought. But with the small-scale approach, there was just a chance ...

The front door was open.

'In here, Inspector!'

Mountfield sounded eerily, horribly jovial. As though this was a dinner party and he the welcoming host.

Warily, they filed into Helen Kavanagh's front room.

The deputy head was sitting on the black leather sofa. She looked oddly composed, almost relieved, even with a sharp bread knife held to her throat.

The man they had been hunting sat next to her.

As to externals, it was the same shambling charm and breezy dishevelment.

'So, you've caught up with me at last, Inspector,' he said with lazy amiability. Then, watchful as a praying mantis, 'Don't come any further.'

There was no chance of bringing him down. That knife would have severed Kavanagh's jugular before they got within striking distance.

Markham lowered himself into the armchair nearest the door. Burton and Noakes stood in the doorway behind him, Doyle in the hall.

'It's over, Harry,' the DI said quietly. 'Or should I say, Howard.'

The other's features momentarily contorted, then the debonair mask was back in place.

'I prefer to go by Harry these days, to be honest. I left Howard Medlock behind a long time ago.'

Markham leaned forward, his voice low and confidential.

'But you didn't really. You never cut the chains which tied you to the past. However far you travelled, you were still the boy who lost his twin brother and mother far too young. However high you reached, there was still a gaping hole beneath your feet. You never forgot Adrian, did you? Your whole life was a mission to avenge him, everything else a pale reality – including Harry Mountfield.'

'Quite the amateur psychoanalyst, Inspector.'

The humorous eyes were suddenly flat and empty, the teasing lilt replaced by a harsh rasp.

'I never forgot what happened. It crushed everything else out of existence.' He flexed the hand that rested on his thighs.

'You know, of course, that Palmer could have stopped what was happening to Adrian. Instead, he looked the other way, the fucking voyeur.'

'We know that JP was bisexual, Harry, and that he loved Ashley Dean.'

A pulse began to beat rapidly at Mountfield's temple.

'Were you in love with Ashley too? Did he lead you on before chucking you aside?'

The tempo of Mountfield's breathing increased, but his eyes were unreadable.

'I think you were ashamed and humiliated. You wanted to wipe Ashley off the face of the earth, not just because of what it would do to JP, but because Ashley represented something secret and degrading – the same thing that led your brother to kill himself.'

Mountfield's lips drew back in a snarl. For a moment, he looked like a mad dog – as though he wanted to bite Markham, to tear the flesh from his bones.

The DI recoiled but did not break eye contact.

'Yes, it's true, Inspector. I wanted to strike at Palmer by destroying what he loved best in the world – like he had done to me.' He gave a mirthless snicker. 'I also aimed to have him take the rap for Ashley's death. Only Dumb and Dumber got in the way.'

'Audrey Burke and Jim Snell.' Markham spoke with cold deliberation. 'Two innocent human beings whom you murdered and defiled.'

'They were prepared to look the other way for money, Inspector.' Mountfield smiled sardonically. 'Though the Berk had a charity in mind, would you believe? With her, it was all about protecting ole JP. Couldn't see the man was a crock of shit.'

'What put Audrey onto you?' Burton shot out.

Mountfield smiled. A slow, chilling smile.

'The eavesdropping bitch overheard me making an appointment with Ashley for an after-hours *rendezvous*. He adored anything which smacked of intrigue, so I had no problem persuading him. I'd nicked Snell's keys and it was all set. Should have been a piece of cake ... but the Berk knew all about the meet... She loathed Ashley of course – he practically mimicked her to her face – so I hinted that I had a sob story of my own and came the repentant sinner.' He smirked. 'Good performance, if I say so myself.' An ugly scowl succeeded the smirk. 'Snell was a different matter. Dug around in my background and opted for blackmail before ending in the slime where he belonged.' With a scornful laugh, he dismissed the caretaker.

'It's over, Harry,' the DI said again. 'Let Helen go. What does she have to do with any of this?'

'She's going to be my last, Markham. My final two-fingers to this self-satisfied, smug, sick world of ours. It's thanks to the likes of her – with her data and her fucking spreadsheets – that no-one really sees the kids anymore ... so the ones who need help the most – the ones like Adrian – slip through the cracks.' He was stuttering now. 'Jabbering on about *empowerment* and *being there for learners* when none of it means a bloody thing.'

'I'm sorry, Harry.'

It was a croak.

'I'm sorry.' The voice was firmer this time. 'That's not

really who I am. The inspector knows that now, but I'd like you to know too.'

It was the authentic Helen Kavanagh, stepping out from behind the mask, thought Markham, and his admiration rose.

The killer's world tilted on its axis. His eyes looked unfocused, childlike.

Markham telegraphed Kavanagh.

Now!

She darted forward with a wild cry, taking Mountfield by surprise.

Arms reached out and whisked her from the room.

The killer sprang to his feet panting, trapped, his eyes now full of hatred. The fox caught in a circle of hunters. It must have been the face that his victims had seen, and it shocked Markham.

The DI stood too, as though they were partners in a gruesome pavane, poised to see the dance to its end.

Never taking his eyes off Markham, Harry Mountfield drew the blade across his own throat.

Later, Markham would have nightmares about that lopsided, half-decapitated poll whose expression of demonic glee, like that of some awful Petrushka, defied bystanders to show pity and seemed to proclaim that he had enjoyed the last laugh.

A fortnight after the unforgettable conclusion to what became known locally as 'the Mountfield Case', Markham and Olivia stood in the garden of remembrance at Bromgrove North Municipal Cemetery, waiting to enter the little crematorium chapel.

It was a cold November afternoon, dank mist cloaking the colonnade memorial wall with its rows of niches. Everything bore a melancholy aspect, nothing more so than the sad little bouquets from other funerals lined up in their serried ranks.

It was the DI's second funeral that week, Jim Snell having been laid to rest a few days earlier at a sparsely attended twenty-minute Humanist service in Bromgrove Woods. There had been no bouquets for the caretaker, just a small bunch of white freesias from the police team.

Markham's gaze rested on the inscription over the stone archway which led from the garden of remembrance to the chapel.

Man, that is born of a woman, hath but a short time to live, and is full of misery. He cometh up, and is cut down, like a flower; he fleeth as it were a shadow, and never continueth in one stay.

So much death.

Very gently, Olivia slipped a hand into his and they walked towards the chapel.

For all its mock-gothic aspect, the chapel's clinical interior was uncompromisingly twenty-first century. Hideous mustard-yellow curtains formed a garish proscenium arch around a catafalque covered in similar drapery. Blinding white floral arrangements stood stiffly to attention atop gilt jardinières, while bilious mauve uplighting bathed the scanty congregation in a lurid hue. A plastic Cross — clearly a last-minute touch — swung from a hook beside the pulpit.

Markham could not remember when he had last seen anything so depressing.

Sliding inconspicuously into a seat right at the back, he

registered some sort of piped music on a loop in the background. 'You'll Never Walk Alone.' How horribly inappropriate for Harry Mountfield, marooned in his own private hell. The canned anthem provided cover for whispered conversations amongst palpably ill at ease mourners, the men imprisoned in dark suits and women awkwardly adjusting fancy hats as though uncomfortably aware that they did not suit the occasion.

Who were these people? Mountfield's – Medlock's – relatives? Gawpers? Press? He locked eyes with Matthew Sullivan in a pew across the aisle. Good to know that Harry's friend had not forgotten him. Helen Kavanagh sat next to Sullivan, lost in her own thoughts, looking somehow diminished and old. No doubt Hope Academy was busily expunging all traces of Mountfield from the record. As if he had never existed.

Suddenly the tinny strains came to a jerky halt and a shuffling behind Markham indicated the arrival of the bearer party. While a hastily substituted soundtrack of Albionini's Adagio in G Minor echoed in the background, Harry Mountfield's mortal remains proceeded to their final resting place.

Markham gave the coffin quick glances, then looked away.

The image of Mountfield's remains inside the coffin tried to enter his head. He shut it down immediately.

For all his revulsion at Mountfield's crimes, Markham felt a sudden fierce hope that the minister on duty that day would be able to speak of him with compassion. Not least for the sake of Olivia who so desperately needed to hear a message of hope amidst the darkness.

An apprehensive-looking elderly clergyman slipped into

the chapel via a side door and waited patiently for the classical track to come to a halt. Markham thought, poor man! How could he deliver the traditional Christian message of hope over the coffin of currently the most hated man in Bromgrove – a killer responsible for three (very nearly four) murders?

'Dearly beloved,' came the uncontroversial opening.

Then there was a dramatic interruption. Markham heard voices, strident and angry, raised in the porch.

'It's a disgrace letting him anywhere near decent folk!'

'Let the bastard rot!'

'What about the victims?'

'Call yourself a clergyman, do you?'

Markham was just preparing to intervene when the clamour ceased as abruptly as it had started. The furious tones died away, shut out by the sturdy chapel door, and the service proceeded without further outbursts.

Clearly shaken, the minister nevertheless managed to deliver the funeral address albeit without mentioning the deceased by name. Afterwards, Markham remembered only the concluding words, 'In my end is my beginning', drawing some private consolation from the thought that somehow, somewhere Harry Mountfield was beginning the world again.

The yellow curtains screened the coffin from view as it slid gently away into the smiling jaws of the furnace beyond.

Afterwards, Markham and Olivia repaired to The Grapes where the team were waiting. Burton and Doyle ducked their heads shyly in greeting, while Olivia twitted Noakes about his unusually dapper appearance. Observing how the DS's ears turned pink, an almost goofy expression softening the trade-mark truculence, Kate reflected wryly that she was not the only one sighing for the moon.

When they were settled with drinks, the conversation turned to Mountfield's funeral, his colleagues listening in stunned silence as Markham described the rent-a-mob disruption of the service.

'That's shameful!' Burton exclaimed disgustedly. 'The man had to be disposed of somehow, and his family had some rights after all. Anyway, what did folk think he was going to do – pop up behind the trolley like something out of a horror movie?'

'You're right, Kate.' Olivia's voice was warm. 'People should let the dead rest in peace. All of them.'

Noakes bit back what he had been going to say. Olivia Mullen was too soft-hearted for her own good. Just as well she was one of the family. The police always looked after their own.

There was a sardonic glint in the DI's eyes which Noakes didn't much care for. Almost as though the guv'nor knew exactly what he was thinking.

Time to drink up ...

Gradually, the conversation turned into more cheerful channels, Olivia congratulating Burton on the news of her permanent promotion to CID.

The DC glowed. 'Yep,' she confirmed proudly. 'And the force is sponsoring me for an M.A. in Gender and Modern Policing.'

She looked across the table at Noakes, bracing herself for the expected put-down, but to her surprise none was forthcoming. Instead the DS's gaze was disconcertingly benign. There had been an uneasy period when she worried that Noakes had somehow detected her thumping great crush on

Markham (for that's all it was, she told herself firmly). But as he sat there mildly quaffing his ale, she told herself there was nothing to worry about on that score.

'And Doyle's had some good news too.' Burton was anxious to shift the spotlight away from herself. 'His secondment's come through.'

'Ah yes, welcome aboard,' Markham said.

He was pleased to see the youngster was looking less love-lorn these days, having apparently transferred his affections from the stony-hearted Sally of yore to an attractive young DS in Traffic who, rumour had it, was not averse to his attentions.

'Things should be better at Hope after Christmas,' Olivia was keen to update them. 'Helen Kavanagh's off to work for the LEA, and they're going to bring in a new executive head. Poor Dave Uttley's on sick leave after that nervous break-down, so Matt's going to take over as the new deputy with Doctor Abernathy as Assistant Head. A fresh start all round.'

'S'pose it'll be business as bloody usual then,' Noakes growled, his mood of sweet reason evaporating. 'You scratch my back an' all that.'

Olivia was determinedly upbeat. 'Not with Matt at the helm.' She added, seemingly inconsequentially, 'Word has it he's quite a useful footballer, you know.'

Noakes was clearly engaged in some sort of internal strug-gle, but his love of the beautiful game prevailed. 'Well, if Sullivan's still there, it's not all bad news then.'

His colleagues stifled their grins. In a changing world, the reactions of DS Noakes were as reassuringly predictable as Bromgrove's bad weather.

Later that evening, Markham and Olivia lay stretched out on the rug in front of their woodburner.

There was something intensely comforting about being indoors in front of a fire on a wild autumn evening, Olivia thought. All the ghouls and goblins at bay.

'A penny for them.' Markham smiled lazily at her.

'I'm just thinking how well it's finally worked out,' she answered dreamily. 'The doc and Matt'll make a great team.'

'I think old Abernathy knew far more than he ever let on about all the sexual tensions swirling around Hope. Looks a new man now it's out in the open and Sullivan's in the clear.'

'Yes, I think he cares a great deal about Matt. But with him it's a case of "the love that dare not speak its name".' She smiled rather sadly. 'Matt has no idea.'

'Between them they'll steer Hope into calmer waters,' said Markham comfortingly. 'You know,' he added musingly, 'Abernathy was right about Helen Kavanagh. He told Kate Burton she was a decent woman underneath it all—'

'Provided you dug deep enough!'

'Something like that. Apparently, she, JP and Uttley engaged in a spot of "creative accounting". Ashley found out and put the squeeze on them.'

'God, how utterly *toxic*.' Olivia spoke with feeling. 'Helen must have hated being under the cosh.'

'Yes, the school was her whole life and she couldn't bear to lose it. Hence the samurai superhead act.'

Behind the big mask and the speaking-trumpet, there must always be our poor little eyes peeping as usual and our timorous lips more or less under anxious control.

'What about you, dearest? Will you go back to Hope?'

Markham scrutinized his girlfriend under half-shut lids.

'Too many bad memories,' she replied wistfully. 'But I won't lose touch with the old place entirely ... Maybe I'll start looking at higher education ... D'you think Noakes'll be too creeped out if I sign up for that new Women's Studies course at the university?'

Markham burst out laughing.

'I think you could convert him to just about anything, if you put your mind to it.'

Chuckling at the thought of his erstwhile Sancho Panza's likely reaction to such an announcement, he drew Olivia closer.

They turned to each other, away from the night and storm and loneliness outside, forming a tableau of perfect contentment.

And the future held no terrors.